1

'Did you get the job?' Kirsty asked as her friend came into the sitting-room of their shared flat.

'No.' Juliette Jordan smiled, her eyes rueful. 'I'm the wrong sex. I should have a crew cut and wear a suit.'

Kirsty giggled. 'I think you'd have problems, with your figure. It's far too feminine — though you've lost a lot of weight recently,' she added worriedly. 'You're working too hard.'

'Maybe.' Juliette flopped down on the sofa, kicking off her high-heeled shoes. 'So much for three-inch heels! I nearly fell off them, and they didn't seem to impress the interview panel one bit. They wheeled out an ancient professor who must have been at least a hundred and two. He kept peering at me, as though he was trying to work out why a woman wanted a job as a surgical registrar!'

Kirsty watched her friend sympathetically. She knew how much it meant to her to step up the next rung of the career ladder — and this was her second disappointment. She tried to think of something consoling to say.

'There'll be other jobs coming up. This was only your second interview — and as for the first . . . ' Her voice tailed away. That wasn't the right thing to say. Neither of them wanted to remember that day.

'I'm really sorry — and — ah — more bad news, I'm afraid.'

One look at Kirsty's face and Juliette knew the worst. 'Not him? He hasn't phoned again, has he?'

'Afraid so — and he's going to ring again at . . . ' She glanced at her watch. 'At half-past seven — in half an hour's time.'

'Right, we won't bother cooking — we're going out for dinner for the whole evening. I'm not speaking to him again.' She was whirling round the flat

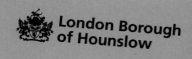
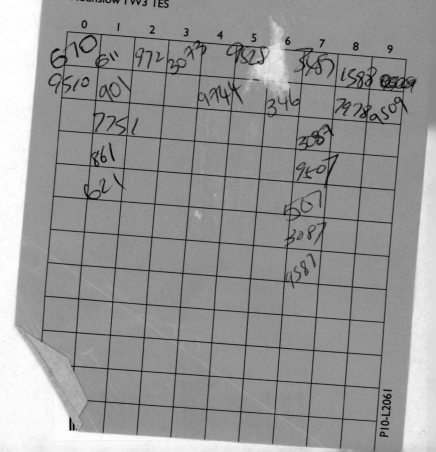

P10-L2061

EDEN IN PARADISE

When Juliette Jordan's parents die at their retirement complex home in Eden Canyon, Arizona, she makes an agonising decision. Knowing their ambitions for her, instead of attending their funeral, she remains in England to attend her interview for a surgical registrar's post. However, calling from Arizona, Josh Svenson criticises her absence and insists that Juliette visit Eden Canyon. She agrees reluctantly, but finds Josh's rudeness unbearable. Then she discovers the shocking truth about her parents . . . but will she also find love?

JOYCE JOHNSON

EDEN IN PARADISE

Complete and Unabridged

LINFORD
Leicester

First published in Great Britain in 1992

First Linford Edition
published 2007

Copyright © 1992 by Joyce Johnson

British Library CIP Data

Johnson, Joyce, *1931* –
    Eden in paradise.—Large print ed.—
Linford romance library
1. Love stories
2. Large type books
I. Title
823.9'14 [F]

ISBN 978–1–84617–681–4

Published by
F. A. Thorpe (Publishing)
Anstey, Leicestershire

Set by Words & Graphics Ltd.
Anstey, Leicestershire
Printed and bound in Great Britain by
T. J. International Ltd., Padstow, Cornwall

This book is printed on acid-free paper

now. 'Come on, Kirsty,' she pleaded, 'we've got to be out.'

'You can't be out for ever. You know he'll ring again. And I can't come — I'm on call.'

Juliette groaned. It would, indeed, have been a rare event for the two of them to be free together. Friends since medical school days, they had been delighted to end up in the same, large, teaching hospital at the beginning of their careers.

Both had worked for two years as housemen, Juliette in surgery, Kirsty in obstetrics and gynaecology. Both were ambitious and Kirsty had just been appointed as registrar at St Kits. Juliette was coming to the reluctant conclusion that she might have to look elsewhere in the country for promotion.

Competition was fierce for jobs at the prestigious St Kits and the awful events of the last month had made it impossible for her to concentrate single-mindedly on job applications and interviews.

The news of her parents' death within two days of each other had shaken her. Her first interview for the post of registrar had been on the same day as the funeral in America. Her agonisingly-difficult decision to stay in England for the interview was motivated by the knowledge that her parents would have wanted it that way. Pride in their only child's achievement had been the driving factor in their lives. All they had wanted was for Juliette to reach the top of the medical profession.

'She'll be the leading woman professor of surgery in the UK,' her father had boasted, and Juliette's heart had sunk with the knowledge that he'd chosen one of the most difficult goals in medicine, particularly for a woman.

At present, she was still stuck on the bottom rungs of the ladder, and that, she considered bitterly, had a lot to do with Josh Svensen and his constant harassment from America.

His phone calls concerning her parents' deaths had been relentless and

4

upsetting. Then, after the funeral, they abruptly ceased and she had breathed a sigh of relief. Now they'd started again.

'What did he say?' she asked Kirsty.

'Not much — just asked to speak to you.' She eyed her friend apprehensively. 'He said it was no good you pretending to be out — he'd find out when you were on duty and ring the hospital again.'

'I'm sure he would, too!' Juliette remembered the earlier call. 'He was so rude,' she'd confided to Kirsty. 'Said I had to go to Arizona immediately — accused me of not facing up to my responsibilities.'

Shuddering, she remembered the other hurtful things he'd said, hearing again the angry exasperation crackling across the Atlantic.

'I've wasted enough time writing and phoning. You either come here — or I come over there and get you myself,' he'd told her. He was so aggressive that Juliette was under no illusion — the owner of that voice wouldn't hesitate to carry out his threat. Anxiously, she looked at Kirsty.

'What am I to do?'

'I think you're going to have to go to Arizona. That man isn't going to take no for an answer — and Juliette . . . ' She spoke tentatively now. 'I think you ought to go, and in your heart you know it, too.'

'But I can't. I've so much work — and another interview next week.'

'You're not doing yourself justice at present with all this on your mind. I know you've tried to block it out — but I don't think you'll ever settle until you find out what's going on. In any case, I don't think you've much choice. He sounded very — positive!'

They both jumped as the phone rang. 'That'll be him,' Kirsty said.

'I can't talk to him. You answer it, please.'

Kirsty shrugged, picked up the receiver, and gave their number. A pause, then, 'Yes, she is — she's here — just a moment.' She held out the instrument and whispered, 'I'm sorry,' before quietly going into the kitchen, ignoring the glare that followed her.

Juliette held the phone as though it would bite her.

'Juliette Jordan speaking.' She tried to keep her tone neutral and calm, but as she listened to the hostile, male voice from the other side of the world, an angry flush deepened her skin. Once or twice she tried to interrupt, but the voice over-rode hers. Finally, there was a pause. She took a deep breath, and when she spoke her voice was acid, corroding her usually-soft, musical tone.

'That is enough, Mr Svensen. Since you insist on keeping up this campaign of abuse, I've no alternative. I'll be with you in the next day or so. Goodnight.'

Juliette was no emotional weakling. She'd coped well with the strains of events during the past month, but her hands were shaking as she replaced the receiver, and her legs felt as though they belonged to someone else. At the same time, she felt a great sense of relief. The decision was finally made — and she knew it was the right one. She followed Kirsty into the kitchen to tell her about it.

★ ★ ★

Exactly forty-eight hours later, Juliette arrived at Sky Harbour Airport in Phoenix. The flight had taken twelve of those hours; the remainder Juliette had used to arrange time off, packing, booking her flight, and cancelling her appointment for the next job interview. That had been hard — to pass up a chance of promotion. Her consultant hadn't been very sympathetic.

'Oh, well, never mind,' he'd said airily. 'Plenty of time yet — you're very competent and hard-working. You'll make a good surgeon one day maybe, but there's no need to be in such a hurry,' he'd ended vaguely.

After that brief interview, Juliette felt resigned. The decision had been made.

Her philosophy in life was to look forward, not back. The career she, and her parents, had set their hearts on didn't allow time for regrets, or much else for that matter.

At the end of the long flight she wasn't too tired and felt more than capable of handling Josh Svensen. As she came out on to the main airport concourse, a grey-bearded man with a weather-beaten face approached her. 'Juliette Jordan?' He held out a huge hand and shook hers vigorously. 'Pleased to meet you. Good flight? We'll reclaim your baggage. The truck's across the way.'

'Just a second.' Juliette disengaged her arm from his firm grip. 'You're Josh Svensen?'

The doubt in her voice evidently amused him and his roar of laughter turned a few startled heads in their direction. 'Lord, no — I'm old enough to be his grandad. I'm Bob Searle. I help out around Eden Canyon.'

'How did you know who I was?'

Juliette warmed to him, but she was still prepared to be suspicious about anything connected with Josh Svensen.

'We have our ways.' Bob was still chuckling as he swung her bags on to a trolley, which he then pushed at breakneck speed through the main exit doors and into the night.

'It's freezing,' Juliette gasped as the cold air hit them. 'I thought Arizona was hot!'

'The nights can be cold this time of the year. You'll be sure to see the sun tomorrow, though.'

'It's good of you to meet me. I could have taken a cab.' She hadn't made any plans, simply left a brief message for Josh Svensen to confirm she was on her way. She'd intended checking into a motel and tackling her persecutor in the morning. But if she had to meet him that night, so much the better, whilst the adrenalin of challenge was still flowing.

Bob had handed her baggage into a large station wagon, its high body dark and gleaming in the airport lights.

'Comfy?' Her chauffeur grinned at her. 'We'll soon be there, so you just settle back and enjoy the ride.'

The vehicle shot out of the car park and within minutes they were bowling along the freeway. For a senior citizen, Bob Searle drove like a boy racer, and the night flashed past, leaving her with an impression of wide roads, garish, neon signs and then, beyond the city, darkness. A faintly-luminous moon showed the stark outlines of distant, craggy mountains, but they themselves seemed to be travelling along a flat plain.

She sighed, leaned back and closed her eyes, prepared to dislike America in general, Arizona in particular, and Josh Svensen most of all. She hated him for his brusque letters and peremptory phone calls, the way he had been continually insisting that she should visit her folks.

Anxiously, she'd written and phoned them, and received cheerful reassurances.

She shouldn't worry; they were fine; she mustn't let anything interfere with her career. They'd love her to visit when she'd got her promotion, but not before.

Josh Svensen's phone call had been put through to the ward where she was on night duty, and there had been no preliminary courtesies.

'Juliette Jordan? It's Josh Svensen.' There was a fractional pause before the deep voice said, with crushing bluntness, 'Your mother and father are both dead. You have to come at once.' No softening, 'I'm afraid I've got bad news,' or 'I'm sorry but . . . ' Just the simple, bald truth hitting Juliette's heart with pounding force. After that, numbness and grief, interspersed by more transatlantic calls.

'The funeral's on Wednesday. You'll be here, of course.'

'No, I can't. I've got an important interview.' Guilt, anxiety, tiredness, gave the words an abrupt, clipped ring which hid her feelings. She knew it must sound callous and uncaring, but she couldn't explain to this antagonistic stranger. She could almost feel the stunned disbelief on the other end of the phone. A lecture followed about filial duty. Juliette put the phone down halfway through.

The final call was on the day of the interview, the voice harsh and grating. 'Miss Jordan, the funeral is over. I hope you're satisfied — and I hope you get your important job. I'll send you the bill.'

He hadn't, although she'd written to ask him for it. There had been no word from him until three weeks later, when he had started the calls again, insisting that she came out to Arizona.

'Here we are.' Bob's hearty voice brought her back to the present. The total blackness outside had given way to pockets of warm light. They were in the well-lit forecourt of a group of low buildings. Tall palm trees lined the driveway and hugh cactus plants flanked an imposing entrance. Juliette was unprepared both for the foreign, exotic look of it all and the sumptuous luxury that met them inside.

'Welcome to Eden Canyon. Hope you'll like it here and stay a while.' Bob ushered her inside, adding softly, 'We were sure sorry to hear about what happened to your parents.' He put his arm round her shoulders and Juliette felt a prickle of hot tears. In a gruffer voice he said, 'I'll tell Josh you're here. Just take a seat awhile.'

There were plenty of soft, leather sofas and armchairs grouped around an underlit fountain which cascaded gently into a marble pool. The atmosphere, relaxed and soothing, was not at all what she had expected.

Neither was the man who now strode towards her. An athletic six foot three inches, Josh Svensen moved with the lithe grace of a powerful tiger. His navy-blue jogging suit and the white towel round his neck indicated a recent workout. His face was deeply tanned, but he was unsmiling as he came up to her.

'So you're Juliette Jordan. About time.' His tone was sharp and uncompromising, and she reddened, hands automatically and fruitlessly searching for pockets to hide in. Now she smoothed them over her hips before clasping them awkwardly behind her back.

'If you're Josh Svensen, you've got some explaining to do,' she countered defensively.

'I have some explaining to do?' He seemed to grow even taller. 'I believe the boot's on the other foot, Miss Jordan. I've had to beg and threaten to get you here — even after your parents died. Wasn't their funeral an important enough reason to come?'

Juliette lashed out without thinking, stung by his accusations. 'There wasn't a lot of point. There was nothing I could do by then!'

A look of incredulous horror passed over Josh's craggy features, and she opened her mouth to defend herself, to explain — then closed it. Why should she bother to explain to this beastly, aggressive man? What did it matter what he thought?

She faced up to him defiantly. 'Please show me to my parents' house. I think we'd better talk in the morning.'

'I've arranged for you to stay the night here, in one of the guest suites. I'll take you to the house in the morning.'

'Thanks, but I'd prefer to go now.'

'Why the hurry? It's taken you long enough to get here. A few hours aren't going to make any difference. There's nothing you can do tonight.'

'I want to go now, Mr Svensen, unless there's some reason, something you're keeping from me?'

He shrugged contemptuously. 'Of course. I was wrong to imagine it would upset you. Nothing could do that, it seems.'

'Would you please mind your own business? I'm here — but you don't have to insult me.' Juliette's voice rose. Reaction was setting in; she felt dangerously close to tears and viewed with horror the prospect of breaking down in front of this particular spectator. 'Either take me to the house or tell me where it is so I can find it myself.' She picked up her suitcase and glared at him, swallowing back her anger.

'I can't let you do that. If you insist, then we'll go now. Can I get you something to eat or drink?' He was the coldly-polite host now, every word like an icicle, and Juliette shivered.

She shook her head. There had been too many meals on the plane. 'No thanks, I'll make a hot drink at the house.' Josh raised his eyebrows but made no comment. He flung his towel on to a chair, picked up her case from the floor and indicated, with a nod, that she should follow him.

They drove along a well-lit road, which followed a circular pattern. He spoke curtly, as though the words were dragged out of him. 'Your parents' house is at the south end of this ring. All the houses face inwards on to a lake, so they all have waterfronts. I'll show you round in the morning, that is, if you're interested in where your mother and father spent their last days.'

'Of course I am,' Juliette replied sharply. She couldn't wait to be on her own, away from the snide, sarcastic remarks and condemning presence of the man by her side. She looked out of the window, partly turning her back on him.

The houses were low ranch-style and, as far as she could see in the well-lit streets, immaculately kept, with neatly-trimmed citrus trees or desert cactus in the front gardens. Her parents had written glowingly-enthusiastic letters about Eden Canyon Adult Living Community — but Juliette had been disapproving.

'Adult living!' Just a euphemism for a retirement complex, where someone made a vast profit out of older people. She hadn't liked the idea of that at all. As the only child of elderly parents, she'd always felt a heavy sense of responsibility towards them, and she'd been amazed when they'd moved to Arizona in spite of her objections.

The jeep drew up outside one of the smaller bungalows. Josh got out and went towards the front door. 'Go on in. I'll bring your case.'

She hesitated on the path, a sudden, chill fear icing her blood. Had she half-expected her mother and father to meet her on the doorstep, arm in arm, as they used to when she visited them at home? She stood, gathering courage to go into the house.

Josh, brushing past her, gave her a curious glance. 'What's the matter? Still hesitating? Might as well take the last step.' There was no friendliness in his face as he snapped on the lights by the door.

At her strangled exclamation of shock, he faced her aggressively. 'What did you expect — that it would be all nice and cosy, just as if your parents were still alive? I told you to wait until morning.'

'But — there's no trace of them — no furniture, photos, ornaments, books.' Her voice rose. 'What have you done with them? Who gave you the right to dispose of everything?'

'You did, by your absence and your total lack of interest in your parents' welfare. I thought you English were family-minded. Heaven help them if you're typical. You don't appear to have cared for them one jot.'

Juliette couldn't believe her ears. The man was insufferable. 'My feelings for my parents are none of your concern. How did you dare clear their furniture out? It wasn't your responsibility!'

She blinked as he moved closer, his deep, blue eyes like hard sapphires, voice grating with fury. 'Now see here, Miss Jordan — don't play the high-handed English lady with me. Someone had to assume responsibility for them. You didn't, so I had to. I can't seem to get that through to you. Someone had to!' he repeated loudly, gripping her by the shoulder.

He gave her a shake as he repeated again, 'You wouldn't — I had to.' The last words were spoken with cold, deadly emphasis as he glared at her, chin out-thrust, breathing ragged.

Not able, or daring to move, Juliette held her breath, conscious of the pressure of his grasp. He was immensely strong and his entire weight seemed to be concentrated in his hands, pressing her into the ground, as though he wanted to crush the life out of her. Her own anger was beginning to drain into tiredness. All she wanted now was to be left alone. She said, 'Let me go — you're hurting me.'

Instantly, he dropped his hands and stepped back. 'I'm sorry, I didn't mean to do that — it's your attitude. So cold — unfeeling.'

'You know nothing about it.' She spoke wearily.

'I only know what I see. Your parents got sick — you wouldn't come. They died — you still wouldn't come. In my book that's pretty unnatural.'

'I don't have to explain myself to you. Why did you make me come? There's nothing I can do now they're both dead.' She congratulated herself on the steadiness of her voice, for it cost an effort.

'A stiff, upper lip. Very British — just as I expected.' There was a sneer in his voice and her anger resurfaced.

'I'm tired, Mr Svensen. Whatever it was you dragged me all this way for, we can discuss in the morning.'

'You're unbelievable. So calm, so collected.'

If only you knew, Juliette thought. She was shaking like a leaf inside, but she met his contemptuous gaze squarely.

'OK, I'll leave you before I say something I might regret.' He moved towards the door.

'Just a minute.' Juliette's clear voice rang across the empty room. 'Have you left anything at all that I can sleep on?'

'There's a floor. The water and electricity are both on and I think there's still a pillow and blanket in the closet. Staying here was your idea, remember, not mine.'

'Did you have to clear everything out with such speed?' she asked bitterly.

'Yes, I did. I've other tenants lined up for this house. Eden Canyon's very popular and I hate to keep folks waiting.'

He was almost at the door when Juliette realised what he'd said. 'You've got *what* waiting?'

'Other tenants.'

'That's impossible — ridiculous. My parents left everything to me — I own this house now. I don't want tenants in it — I'll sell it. Isn't that why I'm here?'

Josh paused, one hand on the doorknob. His next words seemed to give him pleasure and the even tone held a note of triumph. 'On the contrary, you don't own a thing unless I choose to be generous. This house, everything that was in it, is now mine.' He gave an ironic lift of his eyebrows.

'Goodnight, Miss Jordan. I'll see you in the morning.'

The door closed quietly, and a second or two later she heard the noise of his vehicle being driven away. The silence following was impenetrable. She stood in the middle of the empty room, staring at the front door that Josh Svensen claimed was his.

Juliette's medical training had disciplined her to concentrate on one thing at a time. Now she applied that to the man's ludicrous assertion. She decided she'd think about it tomorrow. Right now, a bath, then sleep, were her priorities.

There was no furniture anywhere, but built-in units and fitted, deep-pile carpets made the house habitable. It was spacious and much more upmarket than anything her parents could have afforded in England.

The bathroom was the height of luxury, with spa bath, shower cubicle, mirrored walls and white, shaggy carpeting. She turned on the bath tap and hot water instantly gushed into the pale-blue, marble tub. Soap and bath gel were still on the shelf. These must have been missed by Mr Eagle Eyes, she thought, lavishly upending the bottle into the water.

Totally unprepared for the flood of memories released by the spicy perfume, she sat down on the edge of the bath. It was her mother's favourite sandalwood, a scent for ever associated with childhood. Josh's cruel words came back. *'You don't appear to have cared for them one jot.'* It wasn't true. She did love them, but had never been close to them in the same way as most of her contemporaries were to their much-younger parents. She had been born when her mother was in her forties and her father in his mid-fifties. It often seemed to Juliette, as she grew up, that this unexpected, comparatively late bonus in their lives delighted and astonished them, but also threw them off-balance.

It was Mr Jordan who decided where

the future lay. Juliette was to be a world-famous surgeon! Where this ambition for her came from, she didn't know. A shy and diffident girl, she'd never questioned the logic, nor the wisdom of his choice. If Daddy said that was to be — there was never any argument or discussion.

Her aim was to please her parents and make them proud of her. She was intelligent and hard-working and sailed through college and medical school effortlessly.

Latterly, she had wondered about the wisdom of deciding she should be a surgeon. In that field, it was so much harder for a woman to make it to the top. Juliette envied the easier route Kirsty had chosen.

For a long time, she sat immersed in memories. The bath water went cold, and as she pulled out the plug and watched the water swirl away, it was as though the whole of her girlhood, adolescence, and young womanhood went with it.

Some kind of frontier had been crossed — but the sleep fogging her brain made it hard to think clearly. She fished in her case for the most suitable things she could find — a short, cotton T-shirt — found blankets and pillow in a cupboard and, curling up in a corner of the bedroom, was asleep in no more than a few seconds.

2

The next morning, a clear, gold light filtered round the curtains, touched Juliette's eyelids lightly, and woke her up in a state of confusion. Flinging aside the rumpled heap of blankets, she drew back the curtains to a burst of brilliant light. Early-morning sun reflected silver rays from a lake, its edge only yards from the window. Blue, cloudless skies promised a hot day.

Grey February and the relentless rain in England were already distant memories. The sunshine gave a promise of warmth on the skin which Juliette couldn't resist. Without waiting to find a robe, she went out onto a large patio, where a flight of steps led down to the water. Already, several fishermen were casting lines. It was very quiet, very peaceful. Was this what her parents had so loved — the sunshine, the tranquility?

A cool, 'Good-morning' spun her round to face the broad, athletic figure of Josh Svensen.

'How did you get in?' she demanded indignantly, suddenly aware of her short T-shirt. She pushed her tumbled hair back from her face, unaware that the movement enhanced her shapely figure. Josh Svensen was not unaware, however, and for a second, his blue eyes blazed with a warmth which made the succeeding chill more deadly.

He dangled a set of keys before her. 'I told you last night. It's my house, so I have the keys.'

'You might knock before barging in. Anyway, I don't believe you own this house — you've no proof.'

Josh's eyes narrowed as he looked at her coldly. 'That's no problem.' He added abruptly, 'First of all, though, I promised to show you around.'

Juliette bit her lip. She didn't want to spend any more time than was necessary with this aggressive man.

'You don't need to do that, I can find my own way around. I'd like you to go now, I want to get dressed.' She started to move back into the house, but his tanned, muscular body blocked her way.

'Oh no! I said I'd show you around, and that's just what I'm going to do.' An edge of contempt crept into his already-glacial tone. 'You owe that, at least, to your parents — to see how they spent their last days.'

His capacity to put her in the wrong seemed immeasurable. Trying to speak firmly, she told him, 'I'm sure you don't have the time.' It was a feeble, but desperate, attempt to be rid of him.

'Sure, I've got the time. I've always had the time. It's you who was the busy one, just about every time I phoned you.'

His cold sarcasm and biting contempt was suddenly too much to bear. He seemed determined to attack her — so Juliette decided to defend herself. 'Wait.' She brushed past him and

30

went into the bedroom. Some urgent need to explain and to justify her actions sent her searching through her suitcase. He had followed her into the house and leaned against the door, watching her kneeling on the floor as she pulled out her clothes, scattering them heedlessly around.

Finally, she found what she was looking for, and straightened up. Still kneeling, she thrust a large envelope into his hands.

'Here. Open it and read the letters inside. Since you appear to need an explanation, perhaps you'll find it there — although you already seem to have pre-judged the case.'

'What are they?' Josh raised questioning eyebrows.

'Recent letters from my mother, to me.' With lips tightly compressed, she faced him grimly. She hated letting this stranger see her mother's letters, but she could no longer stand the force of his frigid disapproval.

For the first time since she'd met

him, he looked disconcerted. 'I can't read these — they're personal.'

'I'm surprised you're so sensitive,' Juliette shot at him. 'You don't seem to care about trampling all over my feelings.'

'My impression was that you didn't have any,' he replied angrily.

'Read the letters,' she told him, 'before you pass judgment.'

He took them reluctantly, unfolding the airmail sheets, standing awkwardly in the empty room. Juliette picked up a cotton robe from amongst the things scattered on the floor, stood up, and belted it firmly round her waist. Josh's eyes flickered over her, lingered on the outlined shape of her figure, then moved down to continue reading. Juliette stood by, arms folded, watching him as his attention became absorbed. Once, he looked up as though to ask a question, but she shook her head, indicating he should finish. After a few minutes, he folded up the letters and handed them back.

'I've read enough.'

'Well?'

'I don't understand,' he said slowly.

'I don't either, but can you see now why I didn't come rushing over? Mother begs me not to in those letters — repeating over and over that everything's fine.'

'But why? Why did they do it?'

'Because they love — loved me, didn't want to worry me, I suppose.'

'But surely, after my letters and phone calls, didn't you suspect something was wrong?'

Juliette snorted derisively. 'Your attitude hardly made me want to trust you. You never explained anything, just kept barking out orders to come at once. Who did you think I'd believe? You, a total stranger, or my parents?'

'You're a doctor, according to your parents. Surely you of all people, should have had the imagination to . . . '

'What do you mean, 'according to my parents'?' Juliette's rising anger sharpened her tone. 'Didn't you believe them? What you don't seem to appreciate is that I've always done what my parents wanted me to do. They told me to stay away, so I stayed away. And what on earth it's got to do with you anyway, I can't imagine.' Her blue eyes flashed as coldly as his. He had no right to hold her to account in this way — she'd wished he'd tell her what it was he wanted and then go.

Josh's expression was unfathomable, however. He merely said, 'I'll take you to breakfast. We can talk then.'

'No. I want to know about the house. You promised last night.'

'Breakfast first. I'm starving. You're not on some stupid diet, are you?'

'No, I'm not,' Juliette snapped, resenting his assumption. 'It's too early for me to eat, that's all.'

He snorted, 'Early! It's seven-thirty — practically mid-day here.'

'I've often done a day's work by 7.30. I would remind you that I've barely recovered from travelling thousands of miles yet.' Her rejoinder was acid and he looked at her curiously. Juliette saw that his blue eyes had lost their steely look, but were appraising her with a different expression. 'I'll get dressed,' she said hurriedly.

'OK, I'll wait on the terrace. Don't be long, I'm getting hungrier by the minute.'

'I've told you, I don't want breakfast. Can't you just go? I'll come to your office, or wherever, later.'

'You don't have a choice. You're having breakfast with me, whether you like it or not.' His sudden smile was disarming and, although Juliette didn't want to be disarmed, she could see she didn't have any option but to go to breakfast with him. Josh Svensen was every bit as determined and stubborn as she'd imagined from his phone calls.

'If that's the only way I'm going to get you to talk, I suppose I must,' she said grudgingly.

'Who knows,' he called over his shoulder, 'you may even like it.'

In the airy dining-room, Josh seemed to be on friendly terms with everyone. As they sat down, a pretty, young waitress came to the table.

'Hi, Josh. How are you today?'

'Fine, Sara. This is Juliette Jordan from England. Joe and Margie's daughter.'

Margie! Juliette had never heard anyone call her mother 'Margie'. It didn't sound like her mother at all.

The young girl's face fell. 'Juliette, we were all so sorry about your mom and dad. We loved them. It must have been hard for you.' Juliette was surprised to find tears welling in her eyes. Swallowing hard, she tried to smile. 'Thanks,' she said briefly, and picked up the menu on the table. Through tear-blurred eyes, she stared unseeingly at the seemingly-endless list of choices.

'Don't bother.' Josh's voice was gentle and Juliette saw, with amazement, that his eyes had lost their hardness and were soft and sympathetic. 'Are you hungry at all?'

'No. Coffee and fruit will do.'

'OK, Sara? And the usual for me.'

'You've got it. Be right back with the coffee.' With a smile for Juliette, Sara moved away, but was back almost immediately with iced water and coffee. Juliette sipped hers eagerly, grateful for its calming effect.

Josh left his untouched as he leaned forward. 'It seems I owe you an apology. From those cheerful letters, naturally you'd assume everything was fine. But why didn't you come later — even after the funeral?'

'There didn't seem much point,' she said. This good-looking, confident man could never understand, for it wasn't just the job interviews that had prevented her. Even at twenty-seven years old, her reflex had been instinctive. Her parents had told her not to leave England, and she had obeyed. No, he would never understand. She forestalled his puzzled look by switching to the attack. 'I don't want to talk about that, anyway. Why didn't you tell me what was happening here?'

'Good heavens, woman, don't you think I tried? I begged you to come.'

'But you didn't explain — just kept insisting I should come.'

'Wasn't it enough that they needed you?' He was frowning now.

'But they didn't say that. I never wanted them to come here in the first place. We had a furious row and I told them . . . ' She broke off, remembering, with shame, her hard words. 'I told them not to come running to me if it didn't work out.' She flashed him a defiant look. 'As you see, they didn't!' There was a long pause which Juliette thought would go on for ever — but Sara's arrival with a laden tray broke the silence.

'Here we go,' she said brightly, sliding plates onto the table. 'Eggs, hashbrowns, bacon, muffins and fruit for Juliette. Enjoy your meal.' She bustled away as Josh picked up his knife and fork.

'Do you always eat that much?' Juliette asked disapprovingly.

'It all depends — how I feel, the time of day. Why?'

'It's not exactly healthy.' She sounded prim.

'So?' Josh was laconic, one eyebrow quirking.

She shrugged. 'It's nothing to do with me. It's your life, anyway.'

'You're absolutely right — and it's there to enjoy. You don't look as though you've had much fun lately.' His intelligent eyes looked at her shrewdly, noting the lines of strain round her mouth and eyes. 'You're not much of an advert for your profession.'

'I'm still tired after the journey,' she snapped back, resenting his easy familiarity and minute scrutiny. His hostility was almost easier to bear than his presumptuous concern. She had a sudden urge to be back in England, to be at the hospital, immersed in work.

Her job left little time for introspection, or relationships, and she preferred it that way.

She bit her lip as she looked at Josh. He was incredibly good-looking, the sort of man who would have had most of the female staff at St Kit's Hospital swooning at his feet.

He had finished off his mammoth plate of food, and was spreading toasted muffins lavishly with whipped butter and jelly. As Sara went by, he gestured for the coffee cups to be refilled, and he took his time adding cream and sugar.

Juliette was impatient. 'When you've finished eating, I'd like you to explain about my parents.'

'Sure I will, but first I'm going to show you around. So you can see how it was for your folks.'

'I know how it was. I've never agreed with this ridiculous concept of the 'adult community' as you call it. I'm sorry for these old people, penned up together like battery hens, paying the earth for things like maintenance and security. Being exploited, probably evicted, if they can't pay . . . '

'Hey, just a minute.' Josh's hand had shot out to grip her wrist and she jumped at the contact. 'What half-baked nonsense are you talking? Where'd you get those prejudices from? Just calm down and relax. You're strung up, tenser than a bow string.'

'What are you? A psychiatrist, or something? Let go of my wrist.' She rubbed it as he released her. 'Can we go now and get on with it?' She reached for her bag. 'How much do I owe you for breakfast?'

'On the house — my pleasure.' His grin was ironic.

'I can't let you . . . '

He exploded in exasperation.

'Can't you let your hair down for once? Forget your English reserve. I'll write it off to entertaining clients, if that makes you feel better.'

It didn't, but Juliette had no choice but to agree and follow him out into the warm sunshine. It was a beautiful day and she felt an immediate lift of spirits. The warm air caressed her skin deliciously; if she could get rid of Josh Svensen she might even enjoy a stay here.

They cruised slowly through the wide streets in the high, open jeep. There were people out on the streets, jogging, strolling, or whizzing by in what looked like golf carts. As in the restaurant, Josh appeared to know them all — it seemed he was everybody's friend.

Juliette wondered what his position was at Eden Canyon, and presumed he was a manager. He spoke quickly as he drove, and it was obvious he'd done this sort of 'tour' many times.

'Eden Canyon, as your parents no doubt wrote you, is for older people who want security and the company of their peers. It is not a ghetto for the old, whatever notion you may have. And your battery hen comparison is just crazy. Use your eyes, look around. There's a country club, golf courses, pools, health spas, gymnasia, lakes, arts and craft centres . . . ' He broke off, noting her frown of disapproval. 'What's the matter now?'

'There aren't any children here.'

Of course there aren't. By the time they are fifty-plus, adults are usually happy to give them a miss — except for grandchildren, of course. They can always visit — for a two-week holiday period.'

'What! You actually limit the time they can be here?'

'Not me personally, of course not. It's the rules of the association — it's the residents' free choice.'

'And do you agree with the no-children rule?'

'It's not a personal view. I have an obligation to my clients. It's their wishes that count — not mine. I have a business to run.'

'And I suppose that's all that matters. Profit! Profit for the owners of this place. How can you work for such an organisation?' She flung the accusation bitterly. 'Old people should be with their families, cared for in the community, not in these glorified holiday camps!'

He went very still at her last words and the jeep slowed almost to a halt. 'Lady, how can you be so wrong? And illogical? You're a fine one to talk about family care — 'don't come running to me' was what you said, wasn't it? And I don't work for anyone. I own Eden Canyon.'

The implication of what he was saying made Juliette gasp. 'You *own* it?' she echoed.

'Yes, I do. Is anything wrong with that?'

'Yes, there is. It's pure exploitation. How can you do it?' She looked at the tanned, Nordic face; she knew he could exert charm when he wanted to. All the people he had greeted had practically fallen over themselves to talk to him, and his interest in them had seemed genuine enough. A practised conman, she decided scornfully — who still hadn't explained why he'd assumed ownership of her parent's home.

Completely disregarding her question, he continued the tour, pointing out the beautifully-landscaped grounds, lakes, cacti and lush green lawns surrounding the low, one-storey houses. 'Here's the country club. We'll get out and look around.'

Josh was halfway out of the car before Juliette reached across and stopped him. 'I've had enough of this. I want to know how you came to get my parents' house. You've put me off for long enough. I don't go another step until you tell me.'

Her arm was across his body as she clung on to the handle of the driver's door. A swathe of hair brushed against his cheek. Her eyes were full of frustration and fury. She felt his recoil as she turned her face towards him. 'Tell me,' she said, through gritted teeth.

'OK, OK, there's no need for the melodrama. Can't we go where it's comfortable? There's a very good coffee bar by the pool over there.' He gestured towards a huge, heart-shaped, outdoor pool fringed by tall palms and orange trees, and surrounded by cushioned sun-loungers.

'No, now! I haven't come to lounge around pools.'

Josh sighed and shrugged his shoulders. 'It seems to me that that's exactly what you could do with — but as you wish!' As he spoke, he pulled a sheaf of documents out of his pocket, and tossed them onto her lap.

'Here's your proof. Your father made over the house to me last year. In return, I gave him a cash sum and a guaranteed-occupancy, low rental for life — or your mother's life — whichever event was last. As it happened, they died within days of each other.'

He stated the facts drily and, as she quickly scanned the papers, she saw he was right. A deed of transfer, signed by her father and properly witnessed, was Josh Svensen's legal proof of ownership. The house on the lake, and everything in it, belonged to him.

'I've kept the personal effects, their various bits and pieces. They're at my house. We can go there whenever you like.'

'Thanks for nothing. How did you get him to hand over his home and belongings? I knew these places were out to exploit vulnerable, old people but . . .'

'You know nothing about it,' he answered sharply. 'Wrapped up in your own affairs — your precious career, how could you understand?'

'I'll fight you. You won't get away with this. I'll expose you and your blessed paradise for exactly what it is.'

Josh's laugh was derisive. 'I shouldn't try that, if I were you. You'd be committing yourself to years of legal wrangling. The lawyers would get richer, and you'd be the loser.'

'I wouldn't care.' She was furious. 'I'd at least have the satisfaction of getting you some bad publicity.'

'There's no such thing as bad

publicity. You'd be doing Eden Canyon a favour. We'd have an even longer waiting list for houses. We can sell our units as fast as we can build them.' Josh was complacent now, smiling at her smugly.

She couldn't stand it any longer. The man was infuriating, arrogant, self-satisfied — and, she was sure, dishonest. Her father wouldn't have agreed to hand over his property without good reason, and the only reason she could think of was that somehow, Josh Svensen had deceived him.

He had taken advantage of her parent's vulnerability, and must have exerted a Svengali-like influence over them. He was looking at her now with a faint smile on his curving mouth, his eyes sardonic. She looked away.

How many more properties was he charming out of his customers? She'd make sure that her parents' home was the last he ever grabbed.

Her cousin was a lawyer in her home

town of Bristol, she remembered. She'd phone him right away. Quickly opening the door of the jeep, she jumped down onto the road.

'What on earth . . . ?' Josh leaned across to the passenger side. 'Get back in. I haven't finished yet.'

'I don't want to hear. Nothing you say can possibly excuse what you've done. You're nothing more than a . . . crook!' Turning on her heel, she swung away from the jeep and walked down the road as fast as she could.

Fury gave her speed as she headed back in the direction of what she still thought of as her parents' house. She didn't know whether the phone was still connected but, if it was, she would contact Phil immediately.

She glanced at her watch. It was 10 a.m., about tea-time in England. If she hurried, she could catch him at his office. She had to know her legal rights. Josh Svensen wasn't going to get away with it, just because he was all-powerful in Eden Canyon. If he actually owned all this — she looked around at the lush setting and beautiful houses — he must be immensely rich. He probably thrived on law suits, she decided bitterly. There were few vehicles on the road, so the noise of the jeep was unmistakeable, as it drew up alongside. She quickened her pace but it shot past her before Josh slammed on the brakes with a screech, bringing it to a halt about ten yards in front of her. Juliette stopped as he vaulted down from the driver's seat. She tried to hurry on but he barred her way.

'Don't be such a fool.' He spoke sharply and made a move towards her.

'Don't come near me. You can't charm me, like you do your — clients.'

'You're being ridiculous. Jumping to all the wrong conclusions. Get back in the jeep.' He pulled her roughly towards him.

'Don't order me around. I'm not coming anywhere with you.'

'Right. If you want it straight — here it is. I've been stalling, I admit. It's not very pleasant to have to tell you that your parents lost all their money. There was no way they could have stayed on here without selling the house.'

'Why to you? Why couldn't they sell it and come back home to England — to me?'

'You must know the answer to that one. Can't you accept that they loved it here? They didn't want to go back.' Josh looked as though he had more to say but he hesitated, as Juliette broke in.

'I don't believe any of it and I'm going to fight you. All right, you've got the house for the moment, but I'm going to stay here and find out how and why. My parents did have money — they couldn't possibly have lost it all. Dad was a shrewd investor. I know you're lying.' She flung the accusation at him, rage coursing through her. She wanted desperately to get away, to think, to phone Phil. Turning, she ran back towards the house.

Josh's yell of 'Juliette!', she ignored.

★ ★ ★

'You're not making much sense, Juliette. Just calm down and tell me what's the matter. And what on earth are you doing in Arizona?' Back at the house, breathless from running, she'd dialled the number of her cousin's law firm in Bristol.

'Phil, I'm sorry I didn't let you know I suddenly decided to come. I should have come earlier . . . '

'Yes, I know.' Phil was sympathetic. 'You've had a bad time.'

'It's OK, but I need your help.' Calmer now, she told him what had happened. 'He can't take the house, can he? There must be something we can do. He's nothing more than a con-man — a thief!'

'Hold on. You'll have to produce pretty strong evidence to prove theft. You say he had documentary evidence — proof of ownership?'

'It looks like it — but how do I know if it's valid? And how could Mum and

Dad have lost all their money?'

There was a fractional pause on the line before Phil spoke. 'I don't know, but so far, you haven't got much to go on. Wait a minute — can you stay there for a while?'

'I ought to get back to work — although they've given me three weeks off, if I want it.' She didn't add that the prospect of facing Josh every day was daunting. Instead, she said slowly, 'The sunshine's wonderful, I suppose. Do I have a choice, anyway?'

'I don't think so.' Phil was firm. 'This is what you do. Sort out the relevant documents and fax them to me — straight away. In the meantime, keep your eyes and ears open. Talk to the folks at — what's it called?'

'Eden Canyon. Svensen actually owns it. There are thousands of acres and it's very plush.'

'If he's that rich, why should he want your parents' money? It doesn't add up.'

'That's probably how he got rich

— by exploiting old people.'

'Watch out for paranoia, Juliette. You always were a bit quick to jump to conclusions — usually the wrong ones!'

They both laughed affectionately, instinctively in tune, remembering many a childhood argument together. Phil was her only family now, and she wished he was with her instead of thousands of miles away on the other end of a telephone.

'Don't fly off the handle with — what's his name again?'

'Josh Svensen.'

'Sounds Nordic. Play him along. You'll pick up more if you're a little friendly with him.'

'But Phil, he's hateful; bossy, arrogant and so smug. Must I?'

'Yes you must. What's he like? Old and ugly, or young and attractive?'

'I suppose he's attractive,' Juliette was forced to admit grudgingly, 'if you like the massive, tanned, outdoor Viking-type. Mid-thirties, I'd say.'

'Wow — he shouldn't be too hard for

you to put up with, then. Sounds like every girl's dream. I'm jealous.'

'Don't be silly. Josh Svensen is the last man on earth I'd ever have any interest in, other than exposing him for what he is.'

'If you say so! Give me a number where I can reach you. If you can't handle it, it might be a great excuse for me to escape this dreadful weather. It's pouring down here — and freezing! Count yourself lucky, try to enjoy yourself. Relax — it'll do you good. You take life far too seriously.'

'Thanks. Any more advice, Uncle Phil?'

'No — just have a good time.'

She gave him her number and Phil rang off. His voice reminded her of how far from home she was. She felt lonely in the empty house. She looked in the mirror for company and studied her reflection thoughtfully. Was it true what Phil had said? He'd always had an annoying knack of being right. Certainly, there were frown lines on her forehead and her mouth was tense. Consciously relaxing, she made the lines disappear. Did she take life too seriously?

'Strung up tenser than a bow string,' Josh had said. It was all right for him. And for Phil. They'd made it! Competition in her world was serious, draining and all-consuming.

Not beautiful in the accepted sense, Juliette was pretty and men were attracted to her, admiring her intelligence and fascinated by her challengingly aloof reserve. So far, no man had succeeded in penetrating the barrier that was protection against the wear and tear of emotional entanglements. She'd seen too many colleagues and friends suffering stress and anxiety as a result of broken or one-sided relationships. That wasn't for her. She couldn't afford the time or energy. Anyway, in the past, she'd always worried that any man she went out with would fail to live up to her father's expectations.

Her mind returned to the problem of Josh Svensen. Dealing with him was going to be anything but relaxing. Just then, the door bell chimed, perhaps Josh had come to evict her already? No, it was Bob Searle on the doorstep, with a large box in his arms. Two tanned, senior citizens were hauling furniture out of a small van.

'What on earth . . . ?' Juliette started to ask.

'The boss said for me to bring these round.' Bob dumped the box in the hall. 'China and pans in this one.'

'The boss, I assume, is Mr Svensen?'

'Josh — right first time. He wants you to feel at home here, Julie. Bed, sofa, table, chairs, TV, stereo — should be enough.'

'I can't possibly let him do this,' she protested.

'Why not? The place has to be furnished sometime.'

The furniture looked brand new, and top quality. Juliette's instinct was to refuse it. Then she remembered Phil's advice — 'Play him along.' In any case, Bob and his helpers were already busily installing the furniture indoors.

'Nearly forgot the groceries.' Bob dashed back to the van, returning with yet another carton. 'And here's a note from Josh. See you soon, Julie. Get settled in, then come over for a visit. Mae and I are just across the street and we'd be real pleased to see you. Talk about your folks, too — if you want to, that is.' His voice was gruff and he patted her shoulder.

'I'd like that.' Juliette smiled at him warmly and he seemed relieved. A quick wave and the truck was roaring away. Bob Searle seemed to have no problems keeping a youthful approach to life. He'd called her Julie! How odd it sounded — her father had always insisted on the full Juliette. She said 'Julie' out loud and found she liked it.

She went inside and opened the envelope. The note simply said, '*To help you in the fight. Stay as long as you like — no charge.*' A set of keys was enclosed with the note. The box of groceries contained enough food for a week and there were even two bottles of Arizonan wine! Juliette hadn't even known such a thing existed. She couldn't help feeling excited as she unpacked the box.

The furniture, harmonising in colours of soft, olive green, pink and beige had transformed the house. It was more than habitable — it was luxurious. She wondered if this was Josh's taste or if he had a wife who'd organised it all. Somehow, he didn't look as though he was married although, no doubt, he had a string of girlfriends who would be suitably impressed by his spurious charm.

He doesn't impress me, she decided, but still, she had no qualms about accepting his largesse. Hadn't he taken everything her parents owned? She was certainly going to follow Phil's advice — starting right now.

3

Juliette found Josh Svenson in the Health
Club, which was part of the central
complex where she'd arrived the previ-
ous evening. A pretty, young receptionist
greeted her with the friendly warmth
she was finding common to all the
Americans she's met so far.

'Sure, Josh is in the gym, doing his
daily work-out. Go through, he won't
mind. Perhaps you'd enjoy a work-out,
too?'

Juliette thought that, no doubt, given
time, she probably would, and went
through the double doors indicated. A
short corridor led to a huge room filled
with every conceivable kind of exercise
machine. There was a great atmosphere
of energy and vitality, even though
most of the people in the room were
elderly. At the far end of the
gymnasium, an aerobic class was in

session, a kaleidescope of swinging limbs in brightly-coloured, exercise gear.

Josh was working with weights at the other end of the room. His tanned body looked superbly fit and his muscles rippled as he lifted the weights with ease. As soon as he saw her, he swung them effortlessly to the floor and came towards her, his body glistening with sweat, his hair clinging damply to his head. Juliette couldn't fail to be aware of his virile masculinity and she felt apprehension stir in the pit of her stomach. Josh Svensen looked a formidable enemy.

'I've come to thank you for the furniture. You shouldn't have bothered. I could have managed.'

'No doubt,' Josh said drily, 'but you may as well disagree with me in comfort. I think for now though, we'll declare a truce, as this is your first full day in Arizona.' He glanced at his watch. 'I'm nearly through here. Why don't you go and have a swim? The pool's heated. I'll pick you up at the house in an hour.'

'No. I don't — ' Juliette opened her mouth to protest, but he'd already turned away towards a fearsome machine that looked more like an instrument of mediaeval torture than something that was supposed to do you good.

Josh's bland assumption that she should ignore his poor conduct and calmly agree to go out with him was infuriating, but she gritted her teeth, reminding herself that she had to agree. She was deeply suspicious of his change of mood.

He was capable of cold, contemptuous anger — she'd felt the full force of that when she'd arrived. Now he appeared to be adopting different tactics. Surely reading what her mother had written in her letters couldn't bring about such a change, especially in someone so ruthless? He was certainly up to something. What that was, she had to find out — and that meant that she had to spend time with him.

* * *

It was months since Juliette had been able to concentrate on her appearance. The sun had already touched her skin to a deeper golden peach than usual, and now she washed and brushed her hair until its pale, gold sheen was like rich satin. Making up carefully, she used a darker eye-shadow, to emphasise the deep, dusky blue of her eyes, and chose a softly-pleated, dark, cotton skirt and a cream, silk shirt. By the time she was ready, she looked good, and she answered the ring of the doorbell confidently.

Josh's eyes confirmed what her mirror had shown, and he gave a low whistle of admiration.

'My, you look a different girl. See what Arizona's done already?' In white cotton trousers and dark shirt, he looked elegantly casual.

'Good of you to bother to ring.' She couldn't help the acid comment.

He laughed good-humouredly, throwing up his hands in mock horror. 'Ouch

— it's a truce, remember?'

'You said that. I didn't agree.' She couldn't forget their row that morning, with its unanswered questions. Answers which he was quite plainly not going to give until it suited him. He was irritatingly complacent as he brushed past her into the house.

'It looks right,' he announced with satisfaction. 'More like home. The decor's in the colours of the desert — do you like it?'

'Yes, thank you.' She was stiffly formal. Secretly, she thought it charming, but wasn't going to admit it to him.

He looked at her sardonically, amusement in his blue eyes. 'Can't you relax for an hour or so? You're in Paradise Valley — in Eden, remember?'

'Yes, and what are you? The serpent with the apple?' she snapped back.

He answered quietly. 'If you use your eyes, you'll find very little evidence of snakes in the grass. Shall we go now?'

A silver, open-top Ferrari was parked in the road outside, and she wondered how many more vehicles he had in his fleet! In spite of her antagonistic feelings, her spirits lifted as they came out into the afternoon sunshine. Phil was right — she *would* enjoy herself.

Josh drove the car at a sedate pace, which she suspected was unusual. She studied his handsome profile. His keen eyes were intent on the road, but as if aware of her scrutiny, he turned and grinned at her with such infectious, friendly warmth that she almost smiled back, caught by his charismatic charm.

Instead, she looked away. The way he operated was blatant. Sheer physical trickery. One smile from those beguiling eyes and she'd almost forgotten what he'd done, and was undoubtedly still doing, to his other victims.

Eden Canyon was at the foot of a hill, but the road was flat, a wide, five-lane highway, its monotony only broken by the palm trees which fringed it.

'It's very flat.' Juliette was disappointed.

'Give it a chance. We're down in the

valley. I'll take you up to the mountains later.'

'Later' was ominous and she wondered how long this outing was going to last. How long could she bear to be in the unsettling company of Josh Svensen?

He turned the car into a car park alongside a low, white, adobe building, its small windows protected by ornamental, black, wrought-iron grills. 'My favourite place for Happy Hour. Margaritas for a dollar and all the free food you can eat.'

'I don't want a drink — it's much too early.'

'Yes, you do. It's four o'clock — Happy Hour,' he stated deliberately, as if dealing with a small child. 'When in Rome — '

She followed him into a small bar with a brightly-tiled floor and multicoloured rugs and blankets covering every conceivable surface. Dark, heavy furniture added to the Mexican effect.

As did the tall, dark and very

beautiful girl, wearing a flounced, white, cotton dress, who moved sinuously towards them, huge, brown eyes openly flirting with Josh. He put an arm round her. 'Hi, Anne, this is Juliette — a pitcher of margaritas on the rocks, please. We'll sit over there.' Anne looked disappointed, and Juliette wondered if she was one of Josh's girls. They seemed to know each other well.

'And you've got to sample these,' he said as they sat down.

'These,' already on the table, were thick corn chips with a spicy, salsa dip. 'But,' he added a warning, 'not too many — we're eating later.'

Juliette frowned. 'I didn't agree to spend the evening with you.'

'Maybe not, but you're going to — I hope.'

'I hope,' seemed very much an after-thought and, in exasperation, she asked, 'Are you always this bossy?'

He gave her a lop-sided grin. 'Yes, and I always get my own way — in the end. You're going to find out that I'm one of life's winners, too. You'll have to accept that — so drink up and enjoy yourself.'

If anyone tells me to enjoy myself once more, I'll scream, Juliette thought as she picked up the glass of lime-green liquid Anne had poured. Frowning at the salt-rimmed glass, she winced at the taste of the tequila-based cocktail, and pulled a wry face.

'Don't you like it? It's an acquired taste, maybe, but once you acquire it — you're hooked for ever.'

Taking a second sip, she found it thirst-quenching and pleasant. It seemed innocuous, but already she felt a warm glow spreading through her body. It had been a long time since breakfast and she scooped up salsa dip on a large crisp. Josh's warning came too late and the hot chilli exploded in her mouth and on her tongue. Spluttering, she gasped for breath.

'Ah, sorry. They do a pretty hot dip here.' Josh was laughing at her as she drew a breath and mopped her streaming eyes. 'Have some more margarita.'

'No thanks. I'm OK. Just a surprise, that's all. I like spicy food.'

'Good. You'll enjoy Mexican food then. There are some great restaurants here — I'll show you.'

It was infuriating — his assumption that she would spend time with him. It fuelled her fury even more to know that she had no choice. For her plan to work, she had to be friendly. Making an effort, she said, 'Do you eat out a lot then?'

'Don't sound so disapproving. Yes, I do. You make it sound like a crime. I like the good things in life. Good food, good wine, good cars — everything that makes life pleasant. Yes, and women, too — especially if they're beautiful — like you.'

'The way you live is your own affair. And I'm not beautiful.' She was snappish and regretted it as soon as she had spoken. Josh was deliberately setting out to charm her and, if she was to expose him, he must be lulled into believing she was falling for it. She settled back in her seat; the bar was filling up rapidly, mainly with young people, calling in for a drink after work.

'I'll have another margarita, please.'

'Too late — we're going to move on. It's getting crowded in here.'

Although she resented being swept along so peremptorily, Juliette actually was relieved not to have to drink anymore. One was enough to make her quite light-headed, although she would have liked to stay and watch the crowds. She felt safer, too, where there were lots of people; Josh's 'move on' could be to anywhere!

They came out into the car park and the still-balmy air caressed her bare arms. Rippling her skin like a cat, she luxuriated in the sensuous warmth. It was heavenly, looking up at the deep, blue sky and golden sun which was beginning to orbit towards its Western rim. What had Phil said — relax and enjoy? Well, she'd try, and if it meant

Josh Svensen taking charge, just for this evening, she'd let him, and bide her time.

As she spun the car away from the restaurant, she closed her eyes, leaning her head back against the cushioned seat. The afternoon breeze played with her hair. Drowsily, she was aware that Josh was unusually silent, and it wasn't until he nudged her that she realised she must have dozed off.

'Hey, don't go to sleep. You're missing the scenery.'

Juliette sat up and blinked. The urban landscape had vanished and they were in the middle of a mountainscape.

'This is Superstition Mountain. We'll see the saguaro cactuses, the biggest in the world. We'll stop in a minute.'

Juliette looked at her watch, still sleepy, and bewildered when she saw the time. It was impossible! It was still light, with a brilliant, red sunset splashed across the mountains.

'You haven't re-set your watch yet.'

Josh had stopped the car in a parking area and now leaned across and took her wrist. Carefully, he unclasped the watch, reset the dials, and put it back on her wrist. His touch sent a shock through her, and she snatched her hand away.

'What are we doing here?' she asked suspiciously, as Josh got out of the car.

He laughed, white teeth gleaming in the rosy dusk. 'Get out and have a look — it's a picnic. You know, one of those harmless things that families have all the time — here, and in England too, I shouldn't wonder.'

Juliette was surprised. If anything, she'd expected a seductive night spot with soft music and expensive food — a continuation of the softening-up process. She got out and looked around. The glinting sun she'd seen earlier was now a dull, red ball hovering at the mountain's edge. It still cast a warm light over the hillside, clearly silhouetting the giant saguaro cactuses against the horizon.

'Well?' Josh came to a stand at her side.

'It's very nice. Much more foreign-looking than I expected.'

'You're short on adjectives, you Brits,' Josh grumbled. 'Very nice? It's stupefyingly, amazingly spectacular. Have you ever seen anything like those cactuses before? And the mountains?'

'We've got mountains in England, too.' Juliette was nettled. It was just like him to think his state and his country had a monopoly on scenic grandeur. 'I've said — it's very pretty.' Inwardly, she was captivated, as her eyes lingered on the subtle colours and stark mountain outlines, but she wasn't going to admit it to this conceited American.

'OK. I give in — for the moment.' He laughed good-humouredly, pulling a large hamper out of the massive car boot and placing it at her feet.

He was too charming by half, too accommodating. She almost preferred his earlier abrasiveness. His good-natured affability was hard to resist, and there was something about his body, the way he moved — the way he crinkled up his blue eyes as he watched the mountains. Juliette gave herself a mental shake as he spoke.

'There's a picnic spot just up the hill. We'll take the food up there.' He picked up the hamper and led the way to a clearing where there was a bench and tables permanently set up for picnics. The rosy glow of sunset was fading and the light was becoming softly purple. Josh unpacked the basket and fixed a lantern on one of the canopy supports.

'How many people are you expecting?' She watched incredulously as he unloaded chicken wings, salads, rolls, pates, and fruit onto plates.

'Just the two of us,' he replied innocently. 'I think you need feeding up. But first, we'll have the champagne.'

'You seem to think of everything.' She was impressed, in spite of herself, by the tall, fluted glasses and linen napkins.

'I never do anything by halves.' Josh

popped the champagne cork, and poured the foaming liquid. He handed her a glass with a ceremonial bow, and picked up his own.

'A toast to you, Juliette, and to your stay in Arizona.'

She drank, mesmerised by the enchantment of the setting. The air was still warm, although the sun had disappeared completely, and the light was fading from the pink-streaked sky. It was very quiet and still, as though the two of them were alone in the world, on the top of the mountain. She felt cocooned in a pool of warm intimacy as Josh, shadowy in the lantern light, lifted his glass and drank.

'To you, Juliette,' he repeated softly, touching her hair lightly. He looked deep into her face as if memorising every line, before breaking away to pile more food high on to her plate, until she protested.

'I can't possibly eat all that. What are you trying to do to me?'

'Fatten you up for the kill, of course.'

He was happy and light-hearted. 'Have some more champagne.'

Wordlessly, she held out her glass. Feeling relaxed, she had to keep reminding herself that this man was her enemy and she had to fight him for what was rightfully hers.

He might be entertaining and charming now, but underlying ruthlessness must still be there. She hardened her heart. A full moon had risen and was silvering his hair. He was looking at her quizzically as he poured coffee from a flask into china cups.

'Why have you gone to all this trouble?'

'Why not? You're a visitor. I'm proud of Arizona and like showing it off.'

'Everyone gets this treatment then?' she asked, blue eyes wide and innocent.

'Of course not. They have to be beautiful, too.'

'Don't keep saying that. I told you, I'm not beautiful.'

'You should see yourself from where I'm sitting. Don't you ever look in the mirror?' he asked gently. 'You're beautiful tonight, with the moonlight on your hair — like a silver cloud.'

He meant it. She cleared her throat nervously.

He caught her eyes and held them in a long, long look. Her embarrassment faded in the silence of the night.

Slowly rising, he held out his hand to her. 'There's a look-out spot just over there. We should be able to see the city lights now.' His grasp was firm, warm and natural, as he led her to a concrete observation platform a little way from the picnic spot.

'There!' he said triumphantly. 'What about that for a panorama?'

Golden lights stretched for miles on a carpet of black velvet. The city, set in its grid system of highways, was on a vast plain. Car lights necklaced across the backcloth and some tall buildings were outlined in neon. Secretly, Juliette agreed it was a magnificent view, but didn't want Josh to see she was impressed.

'Just like London by night,' she said airily. 'Get high enough and any city in the world looks like that.'

Josh was very close to her and she felt him stiffen as he let go of her hand. 'Well,' he told her resignedly, 'it seems you are determined to remain unimpressed. Perhaps we'd better go back.'

Juliette was conscience-stricken. The barriers she'd erected were solid to the point of rudeness. The man had entertained her and she was being boorish and ungracious. 'I'm sorry,' she apologised. 'I didn't mean to be rude. It's just that — ' She faltered.

Why didn't she tell him how much she despised him, despised what he had done to her parents, and what he stood for? But all she could think of right now was his close proximity and the sense of loss she felt when he had removed his hand from hers. A strange lethargy kept her rooted to the spot, and a slow heat was spreading through her body. Dizzily, she leaned back and found the support of Josh's broad chest. His hands came up to her shoulders and he turned her gently to face him.

'Don't,' she breathed, but knew inevitably, as he looked at her face bathed in the moonlight, what would happen. Her heart began to thud painfully in her chest as he bent his head. His lips found hers softly, then with increasing pressure.

Juliette was staggered by the treachery of her responsive body, her mouth yielding before she could even think of pushing him away. His grip tightened as he gathered her closely to him, and for a second she was overwhelmed by sensation as his mouth moved away from her lips to caress the pulse at her throat.

As his lips left hers, sanity returned. How dare he? This was the man who had destroyed her parents and was now trying to win her over with cheap seduction. What a weak fool she was. She'd been taken by surprise, or maybe it was the champagne. It was a long time since she'd allowed any man near her and this one contact with Josh Svensen had set her on fire. She took a deep breath and pushed him away with such force that he loosened his hold.

She gasped out, 'Don't think you can get round me that way! I'm not vulnerable, like my parents or all those other old people.'

Josh blinked for a moment, then his dark eyes flashed, and he reached for her — not tenderly this time, but angrily. He crushed her to him and she was helpless to withstand the fierce pressure of his mouth. He was so strong that all she could do was to try to remain still, but her body began again to respond. Everything else went from her head except the exquisite pleasure Josh's nearness was giving her.

Despairingly, she felt her own arms reach up to clasp behind his neck, shivering with pleasure as her fingers touched the soft hair. For minutes, they stayed locked together, then Josh lifted his head, his eyes glittering in the light of the moon.

His voice was husky. 'You are beautiful!'

That flattering lie again — she caught her breath, angered by his words, and ashamed, now, of her response. She wasn't beautiful. How could he think she was? Beauty was something unique, special — a quality few possessed. It was all part of Josh Svensen's seduction game.

Breaking his hold, she stepped away, still trembling from the aftermath of the feelings that had swept through her. It couldn't be true. She was wildly attracted to him, yet she hated him with all her being for what he had done to her family and what he stood for. With an anguished sob, she turned and started to run back to the car.

He caught up with her easily, grasping her arm to stop her flight.

'Let me go,' she gasped, struggling to free herself, feeling heat soaring through her flesh at the touch of his fingers.

'Where to?' He laughed. 'You can't

go anywhere without me, and I've no intention of leaving you on the mountain all night. Stop behaving like a child, and come back and help me pack up the picnic. I'll take you back then, if you insist, although it seems a shame to waste the moonlight.'

He pulled her around to face him and, as the moon went behind a cloud he became a huge black shape, reaching out to engulf her.

She tried to step back, but he still held her arm and drew her closer.

'Don't,' she said sharply into the darkness, fearful for a second, as he loomed nearer. What a fool she'd been to go there. She had no idea where they were, it was lonely, and Josh was very powerful. Her imagination began to run riot. What had he brought her there for in the first place? She was totally helpless, not a feeling she enjoyed, and her blood was still pounding from the remembered recollection of his mouth on hers, his strength and passion. What had she stirred up by her response? She held her breath, not daring to move, then exhaled in relief as Josh's anxious voice came out of the darkness.

'Juliette, are you all right? The moon'll be out again in a minute, and you can see the light of the picnic area over there. You're not frightened, are you?'

'Of course not,' she lied. 'Just startled by the darkness. You may be able to see in the dark, I can't.'

'Take my arm. I'll lead you back to the car. I can fetch the picnic things down.' He held her gently, drawing her arm through his and stepping carefully down the rough track towards the car. As delicately as if she was bone china, he put her into the passenger seat.

She protested, 'I'll help with the things. I'm perfectly all right.'

'That's not necessary, I shan't be long,' and off he sprinted, leaving her alone.

Glad to be away from his presence, she could feel anger returning. He was playing with her — amused, no doubt, by her momentary panic, pleased with himself that he had distracted her from her main purpose. Yet, as soon as he had sensed her fear, his mood immediately changed and he appeared to be genuinely concerned.

Appeared! That was the key; role playing must be his forte and, she had to admit, he was an excellent actor. He'd laid on a fine show for her, acting the charming host to perfection. He'd only spoiled it by going over the top and kissing her. He was carried away by his own performance, Juliette thought resentfully, as he came to the car to stow the picnic gear away.

He slid his athletic length into the driving seat and looked at her anxiously. 'Are you all right?'

'Yes, of course, I am. I just want to get back now, please.'

'It's still early. Why don't we go into Phoenix for a drink? I know a lovely little — '

'I'm sure you do,' she cut in quickly, 'but I've had enough to drink and I'd like to go home.'

He shrugged, turned on the ignition and swung the car round to face down the mountain road.

Neither of them spoke on the journey back and Josh drove much faster than before, pulling his powerful vehicle round the bends on the narrow road at what Juliette thought was an alarming speed. Glancing at him briefly, she saw that his face was taut and set, a deep frown line on his forehead adding to his handsome ruggedness.

His capable, brown hands showed white knuckles as he gripped the steering wheel. He asked whether the open top was too cold for her, in a politely formal tone, and although the night was growing chilly, she shook her head. The air was cooling her, blowing away the memory of her response to Josh's embrace. She thought, with relief, that his act was over. It had failed and he would have to account for his actions — but she could wait.

Phil's advice had been so right! By

biding her time, she could learn a good deal. Josh Svensen was already revealing himself to be a sham. Capable of good performances, yes, but unable to sustain the act!

Outside the house — his house, she must remember what he'd done — he opened the passenger door for her, but his face was unsmiling as she got out.

'Thank you very much for the picnic,' she said dutifully.

He gave her a strange look, but the expression was grim. 'Not at all.' He matched her formality. 'I hope you enjoyed some of it, at least. No doubt I shall see you in the morning.'

'Yes. You still have some explaining to do.' Juliette was frosty, and saw anger in the steely eyes, tension in the clenched fists.

He made the merest move towards her, then checked himself, simply saying quietly, 'If you call in at the office, my secretary will make an appointment for you to see me. Good-night.'

He was gone before Juliette had time to unlock the front door, the only reminder of his presence, the fading purr of the car's engine.

Once indoors, she stood irresolute; despondent when she should have been cheerful, restless when she should have felt calm. Wasn't that what she wanted — an explanation, to be on her own, with the promise of a business-like footing?

The afternoon and evening with Josh had been disturbing and frightening, and the fear had come from her own irrational behaviour as much as anything. The evening had also held enchanted moments — she was honest enough to admit that. Now it was over, there was a sense of anti-climax.

She wandered about the house, tidying up, re-arranging cupboards. That very soon palled. She went into the sitting-room and flicked through the innumerable TV channels. That was even worse!

At first, she took the chiming bell to

be part of some inane advertisement, but when it rang again, the commercial for cat food on the screen just didn't fit. She switched off the set, wondering who it could be at the door. Her heart did a double-quick thump, as she realised it might be Josh. Instead, it was Bob Searle on the door-step, holding a covered dish in his hands.

'Hi, Julie. Mae's sent these cinnamon rolls over for breakfast tomorrow and says why don't you step over to our place now and sample one, freshly baked, with a cup of coffee?'

'I'd love that, Bob,' Juliette said eagerly. 'Are you sure it's not too late?'

'Never. I know most folks in Arizona go to bed early, but Mae and I are from California, so we're still night birds, I guess.'

She slipped on a short coat, locked the front door, and followed Bob a short distance up the road, to a house similar to, but larger than, the one her parents had lived in.

Mae Searle was a trim and lively

senior citizen who looked so youthful that she always had trouble claiming her rightful discounts in the stores. She gave Juliette a hug.

'You're like your mother,' she said simply, as she led the way into the elegantly-furnished sitting-room. Then, after a warning look from her husband she went on, 'Don't mind me — we'll talk about them if you want to, later maybe, when you're settled in.'

Juliette nodded, and took the coffee and rolls Bob passed her. 'I'd like to — in a day or two. I'm still getting used to — all this. It's not what I expected.'

'Didn't your mother write about it?' Mae asked.

'Yes — but — I don't know. Maybe I hadn't thought it through. It's all very different from what I'd imagined.'

Bob chimed in eagerly, 'It's the best community in the state — or anywhere for that matter, I shouldn't wonder. And most of that's because of Josh.'

'Josh?' Juliette queried blankly.

'Now, Bob, don't go betraying

confidences. You know how Josh feels about it.' It was Mae's turn to shoot a warning look. Juliette wanted to ask more, but the Searles adroitly changed the subject, and obviously weren't to be drawn on Josh Svensen that night.

They were both Anglophiles, and asked eager questions about England. They wanted to know all about Juliette's work at St Kit's, and what the hospital was like. Their friendly hospitality warmed Juliette's heart, and, as they chatted, she felt the tensions of the evening die away. For the first time since arriving in Arizona she felt relaxed and at ease.

The doorbell chimed as they were in the middle of a lively discussion about British and American attitudes to each other.

'I'll get it.' Bob got to his feet. 'Don't go away, Julie, I want to tell you about our trip to Stratford and York.'

Juliette laughed. She didn't want to go away; she was enjoying talking to the Searles too much.

'Don't you get Bob on Stratford, he'll never — ' Mae broke off. 'Hi, Josh, how nice to see you. We've got Julie here and we're having a great time. Come in and join us.'

Framed in the doorway, filling its space, was Josh — the last person Juliette expected, or wanted to see.

He checked his step into the room when he saw her, sitting comfortably curled up in the corner of the Searles' big sofa. 'Julie?' he repeated, looking at her incredulously.

'Julie, yes.' Mae grinned at him. 'Suits her much better than Juliette, we think. You don't mind, do you dear?' she asked, half-apologetically.

Juliette hesitated. 'Well, no — I quite like it. Sounds like a different me.'

Josh's clear, blue eyes glinted with amusement, and he sat down on the sofa, very close to her. A slow smile spread over his attractive features as he looked into her eyes.

'Well, Julie it is then — we can make a whole new start on that.'

4

Juliette couldn't help it. Josh's charm was infectious and she was, surprisingly, pleased to see him. In the Searles' luxuriously-comfortable sitting-room, he didn't appear at all threatening. She smiled back.

Mae made a great fuss of her new visitor, jumping up to get coffee and cinnamon rolls. 'You don't come often enough,' she chided. 'We're always happy to see you.'

'I know that, Mae, and I love to come — but I've been busy lately.' He changed the subject quickly. 'So, Juliette's — Julie's — making herself at home. You must meet more of my 'old folks'.' His eyes glinted mischievously, as Bob punched him on the shoulder.

'Hey, less of the 'old folks,' young Josh, or you can do your own furniture-hauling next time.'

'You know I don't think of you as old folks.' He glanced at Juliette, who flushed.

'Mae makes me feel at home,' she protested. 'I haven't had time to adjust yet. I've never seen anything like Eden Canyon. It's so big, and well laid out. We don't have anything like it in Britain.'

'I guess it's hard, with your climate. We've got practically all-the-year-round sunshine here, and it makes a big difference,' Bob chimed in. 'Can be too hot, in the summer. It was almost impossible to live in Arizona before air conditioning. Even now, you jump from car to house pretty smartish in July and August. You really can sizzle eggs on the pavements in Phoenix! You've just hit the right time of the year, Julie.' He beamed at her, wide and friendly.

Everyone smiled such a lot, it was hard not to smile back. Juliette contrasted it with London's grey, February streets, weary people on trains and buses. Sunshine really did make a difference!

'I've just had a wonderful idea.' Mae spoke enthusiastically. 'Why don't we plan a trip for Julie? She ought to see something of the state, apart from Phoenix and Eden Canyon. You should come too, Josh, it's ages since you had a break. I know — the Grand Canyon! You can't possibly leave Arizona without seeing it — its the number one wonder of the world. It's only a day's drive, and the route is so pretty.

'Would you like that, dear?'

Faced with such enthusiasm, Juliette could only nod her head. Why did everyone seem so pleased with life? Had her parents been the same, here in Eden Canyon? She remembered, in England, they'd seemed constantly harassed and dull-faced, a worried frown always creasing her mother's forehead. She wanted to ask Bob and Mae about them, but felt disinclined while Josh was there.

He stood up. 'Thanks for coffee, Mae — wonderful rolls, as usual. I just stopped to ask you — ' He sounded unusually diffident as he glanced towards Juliette.

'Could you look in on Len and Barbara? I'm a bit concerned about them. They tell me everything's fine, but I feel there's something wrong. They're a mite over-cheerful for my liking. Maybe they'll open up with you, Bob — or Mae.'

'Sure will. We'll look in first thing tomorrow.'

Josh looked relieved. 'Thanks, and can you do one more thing? Fix up that trip to the Grand Canyon — and count me in? I'd like to be there when Julie sees it.' With a big bear hug for Mae, and a clap on the shoulder for Bob, he was gone.

There was a vacuum after he'd left, and Juliette felt it was time for her to go, too. She swung her legs to the floor.

'There's no need for you to leave,' Mae said. 'Sit down.'

Bob nodded. 'It's always quiet when Josh goes. He's got a big presence — in lots of ways. There's lots of folks here

95

who should be grateful to Josh Svensen.'

'Shush, Bob. You know how things are.' Mae nodded towards Juliette.

'Who are Len and Barbara?' Juliette asked, to break an awkward pause.

'Oh, just a couple up the road, in the house with the wagon wheel outside. They're a bit older than us. They've gone into their shells rather, lately.'

'Maybe they just want to be on their own,' Juliette suggested tentatively. 'My parents weren't very sociable.'

The Searles looked astonished. 'Can't be the same folks we knew, then.' Bob shook his head. 'Never known such a happy-go-lucky pair. That was when they first came. Life and soul of Eden Canyon, they were. We all loved them.'

'My parents?' Juliette found it unbelieveable.

'Margie and Joe joined everything there was. Golf, swimming, art classes. You name it — they did it.' Mae was firm about it.

'Marjorie and Joseph?' Juliette said wonderingly. 'What happened to them?'

'Eden Canyon, I guess. Of course, later, things weren't so good, but they had some good times, you can be sure of that. I'm truly sorry about — well — what happened. I'm sure you don't want to talk about — rehash all that again. Such a shame you couldn't come to the funeral.' Mae patted Juliette's hand, then said briskly, 'And now I'll look out some brochures. You're going to love the Grand Canyon.'

Juliette finally got back to the house an hour later, Bob insisting, with old-fashioned courtesy, on escorting her. 'Though there's no worries here on that score. There's a continual security patrol, so everything's safe as houses,' he assured her.

It was a long time before Juliette slept, although the big bed Josh had provided was the last word in comfort. She had so many things to think about, so many impressions to absorb. Much had happened since she left London, yet she still couldn't figure out what had befallen her parents.

Bob and Mae seemed to assume she knew the whole story, whatever it was, and it seemed ridiculous that, as their only daughter, she didn't know anything about her parent's last months. Now, she felt awkward about raising it with them. It was Josh who held the key — and he was taking his time unlocking the door!

Meanwhile, Eden Canyon intrigued her and, next morning, she was up early, anxious to look round herself, without the presence of Josh Svensen. Juliette realised she would have to do something about transport — perhaps hire a car, or get around in one of the buggy-type, golf carts everyone seemed to use.

The main complex seemed the sensible place to find out more. On her way, she passed a house similar in design to her parents, but with a decorative wheel outside. Len and Barbara! Juliette wondered what their problem was, and why Josh was so interested. Stopping to admire the cacti in their desert-style garden, she glimpsed a white-haired couple sitting on a patio over the remains of breakfast. Juliette adopted the friendliness of Eden Canyon and waved. They waved back, but didn't call out, and she went thoughtfully on her way.

The receptionist at the complex, displaying her name — Susan — on a lapel badge, greeted her like an old friend, 'Hi there, Julie. You want to see Josh?'

'That's the idea. He told me to make an appointment, through his secretary.'

Susan frowned. 'Doesn't sound like Josh — he's not usually so formal. I'll give Gina a buzz.'

An elegant, dark-skinned woman came out into the foyer, her brown eyes suspicious. 'Juliette Jordan? I've a message from Josh. He's tied up all day, but he'll meet you at four o'clock to discuss your problem. He says, use the facilities here, or take a car, if you want to explore.' Her manner was chilly — it was the first time Juliette had met anything but warm friendliness.

'Thanks, I can manage without a car,' Juliette replied, put off by her manner. 'I'll be back at four.'

Gina consulted a note-pad. 'No, he's calling for you at the house.' She turned and walked away, high heels clipping across the marble floor.

Juliette raised her eyebrows, and Susan gave her a conspiratorial wink. 'She's moody today. She thinks she owns Josh, and probably resents him taking an interest in you.'

Juliette was taken aback by the receptionist's disconcerting frankness, although, apart from Gina, that seemed the norm at Eden Canyon. The other exception was Josh himself, who was still stalling, leaving her to kick her heels all day. Well, there was lots she could do. He'd miscalculated if he thought she was going to wait around, twiddling her thumbs. 'Are there any shops nearby?' she asked Susan.

'Why, sure. There's a small shopping mall not far away, and it's got just about everything you'll need. Look — take a buggy — there are some spare ones around.' She indicated a row of carts outside, all marked with the same logo — a saguaro cactus underneath a palm, and the proud name 'Eden Canyon.'

'You just take it where you want to go, bring it back, or leave it for someone else.' Juliette looked doubtful, but Susan persisted. 'Go on — they're fun. I'll show you how to use it. It's simple.'

Juliette found she loved it! Relaxed, enjoying the sun and air, she drove the buggy cart to the mall, found an office equipment shop with a fax, and sent copies of the documents Josh had given her to her cousin, Phil. Instant action — that's what she needed! She would take advantage of all the facilities too, and find out as much as she could about Josh and his activities. What better place to start than the health and fitness club? That seemed to be the focal point of activity.

⋆　⋆　⋆

When Josh arrived at her front door promptly at four o'clock, Juliette felt better than she had done for years. A workout, followed by a swim and sunbathe, had loosened her limbs and made her conscious of how little she'd used her whole body, physically, over the past year. There was a glow about her which Josh was quick to appreciate.

'You look better every day! You won't need long before you're a different person.' He touched her cheek, his coldness of the day before apparently vanished. 'You're blooming like a desert flower.' He leaned towards her and gave her a friendly kiss on the cheek.

Juliette was suspicious, but she'd so enjoyed the day, in spite of her frustration, that she fell in easily with Josh's mood. After all, she kept reminding herself, isn't that what I'm supposed to do — find out all I can about Eden Canyon?

She'd talked to lots of people at the health club and, without exception, they all appeared to be loving their lives there. Not one word was uttered against Josh or his management of the complex. Now, handsome, standing smiling on her doorstep, he looked completely carefree.

'I presumed we would talk at your office. It is business, and that's what you said last night.' She was still prepared to be on the defensive.

'Last night was last night. Today's a different story. I've been working since five o'clock this morning, and I'm closed for business right now. I've come to take you bowling.'

'Bowling!' Juliette exploded in surprise.

'An American custom. You've got to sample everything.'

'But — I've never — '

'I'll show you. Don't worry — and you're wearing just the right gear.' His eyes swept over her slender figure, in dark cotton chinos and silky sleeveless top. 'Bring a jacket — it may get chilly later.'

She hesitated. He was doing it again — bulldozing her! But bowling did sound fun!

★ ★ ★

He stood very closely behind her, and her senses fluttered. She smelled the piquancy of his aftershave, mingling with his clean, outdoor tang. His left hand was round her waist, his right guiding her heavy bowl. 'Try now.' He reluctantly stepped away. 'Step up, and follow through — aim straight for the pins.'

Juliette released the ball in a swift, economical movement, sending it pelting noisily along its alley. All ten pins scattered and fell, and she felt almost as elated as when she'd passed her finals!

'Beginner's luck!' Josh said, just as pleased, and sent his own bowl skittering down for a nine. After an hour, he called a halt.

'Just one more,' she pleaded, caught up in the energy and excitement of the game, her hair swinging round her flushed cheeks as she curled a bowl in her fingers.

'There isn't time. I've booked a table for dinner at The Buttes.'

'Dinner? The Buttes? Why?'

'You still need feeding up; there's a fancy hotel at The Buttes overlooking the city. It's got great views.'

Juliette forgot that Josh was her adversary. 'I'm not dressed properly for a fancy restaurant.'

His eyes appraised her again. 'You look lovely. And anything goes here — it's how you are that counts.' He tucked her hand in his as they left the bowling alley.

The hotel in the Buttes was an amazing place. Built between two hills, it looked more like a millionaire's fantasy than a hotel! A waterfall cascaded down the rocks, and cunningly-concealed lamps highlighted the surrounding palms and desert plants.

Inside, it was all modern elegance, and when Juliette and Josh were seated in the restaurant overlooking the swimming pool, she decided it was indeed fancy, but pleasantly informal and comfortable to be in. The menus were huge, and Juliette was alarmed by the size of the portions being presented at adjoining tables.

'Steak's the thing in Arizona . . . ' Josh was running his eye down the list. 'There's a good Californian Cabernet, but I expect you'd prefer chicken or fish — and white wine?'

'You're right, but go ahead and have steak if you want.'

The waiter came for their orders. 'Two lobster specials, green salads, and a bottle of Californian Chardonnay.' He turned to Julie. 'Will that suit you? You don't mind Californian wine?'

'I'd love to try it — and lobster would be great.' She was touched that Josh had deferred to her tastes. With his appetite, he'd surely have preferred a huge steak and fries!

He leaned forward to pour the wine. 'To Anglo-American entente — especially yours and mine.' He lifted his glass to her, his mouth curving upwards in a warm smile.

Juliette drank the fragrantly-honeyed wine and returned his look. Still exhilarated from the bowling game, she said frankly, 'Josh, I'm enjoying this. I can't believe that only a few days ago I was in London. Everything's so different. I do like it here — but I just can't ignore my situation.

'You tell me my parents lost their money — just like that! I want to know how and why — you must understand. What happened?' He captured her hand in his, gripping it tightly when she tried to pull away, and her voice trembled a little as she felt the warm pressure of his fingers.

'I'm fighting you over my parents' house, so why do you keep taking me out like this?' She spoke knowing her ambivalent feelings confused her. She ought to hate this man, but, as well as the strong pull of physical attraction, she was finding it hard to resist liking him.

She was enjoying his company, even beginning to relax with him, and it was difficult to remember that she was supposed to be just playing along, acting on Phil's advice.

His voice was low, and she had to lean forward to hear him. Her hair fell forward, and he held it back as he spoke.

'I wish you'd trust me, Julie. I know it's difficult because we got off on the wrong foot. You're mistaken about me — and Eden Canyon. I'm not out to make a fortune by exploiting vulnerable and elderly people — you must believe that.

'Your parents are dead. They sold the house to me because they were short of money. Your father made some bad investments. The stock market's pretty volatile, and he got it wrong. It's happened to lots of people. He was just unlucky, I guess.'

'But he didn't have to play the stock markets. He and Mum were quite well off. So what caused it all?'

Josh's eyes narrowed and he glanced away from her. 'When people are retired, they find different things to do. The stock market's a kind of hobby. Harmless enough.'

'Not in their case, obviously,' Juliette shot back.

'Maybe not, but that's how it was. They were short of cash, so I bought the house. That's all there was to it.'

Juliette wasn't convinced he'd told her the entire truth, in spite of his firmness, but at that moment the waiter arrived with the fish, and Josh let go of her hand. He waited until they'd been served and then, before she could carry on, he said swiftly, 'As to why I want to take you out, that's surely obvious to even the dimmest wit — and you're no dim-wit.'

He looked at her quizzically.

'I like you, that's why. I like to see you opening up, blooming like a desert flower. I like to see the tense, strung-up girl, who arrived here spoiling for a fight, relax and enjoy life. That's what it's about — live for the present and future — not the past. Let it go, Julie. Honestly, it's the best way.'

She bit her lip. Could she trust him? Did he really like her, or was it still all part of the buttering-up process? She was uneasy and returned to the attack. 'But why pester me to come out here? Why didn't you leave me in London to get on with my career?'

Josh took a mouthful of lobster. 'You had to come some time, to see where your parents had lived, and to clear up their personal things. Is your career really so important?'

'Yes.' She spoke positively, but wondered, for the first time, if that was true.

'To you — or to your parents?'

'My p . . . me, of course. This lobster's delicious. But you're still ducking my questions. Did you bring me to Arizona just so you could lecture me on my moral defects as a daughter?'

Josh placed his knife and fork carefully on his plate, although there was still plenty of lobster left. 'I think,' he said slowly, 'I asked you here so that I could dance with you.'

Before she could protest, he'd scooped her up into his arms and they were moving to the slow, languid beat of the band. The top of her head barely reached his shoulder, but he moulded her to his tall body as though she were an extension of himself. She loved dancing, but had little time for it in her busy life. Now she melted happily into the sensuous rhythm of the dance music.

Josh whispered, his lips brushing her cheeks and hair, 'That's the way — at last you're beginning to relax.'

They finished dinner and danced again, moving, whenever the music was appropriate, in the old-fashioned way, close together! When they weren't eating or dancing, Josh entertained her with stories of Arizona's Wild West history. He spoke with love and affection of his own family, his parents and sisters, all living in New England.

Juliette shelved the questions surrounding her mother and father. There would be time enough to act, she decided, when she'd heard from Phil.

'Do you see much of your family?' she asked, unaware of the wistful note in her voice.

'As much as I can. They're great fun to be with. I'm trying to persuade them to come out here permanently, but' — he shrugged — 'they're still attached to Connecticut. Maybe when they're older, and after a few more New England winters, they'll head for the sunshine here. I'd dearly love to have them at Eden Canyon.'

'Have you always got along well?' Juliette was fascinated by other people's families and, subconsciously, she supposed there was a certain amount of envy in her interest.

Josh was so extrovert and confident. Maybe the security of his family had given him these qualities.

'Mostly. Well, always, apart from one hiccup.'

'What was that?'

There was a long silence. 'Nothing, really — do you want a liqueur?'

'No, thanks. It was a lovely meal, though. Tell me about — the hiccup.'

Josh sighed. 'I shouldn't have mentioned it — it's not very interesting.'

'Yes, it is. Tell me.' Juliette was intrigued.

'Well — ' He spoke reluctantly and, for once, his casual confidence seemed to have deserted him. 'It's all blown over now, but we had a great bust-up when I — when I quit practising medicine. They wanted — '

'You're a doctor!' Juliette was astounded. 'What are you doing in Eden Canyon, then? What a waste of — of — training. Why did you give it up?'

He leaned back. 'It's a long story, and I don't want to go into it now.'

'Why not? You can't drop that on me and leave it unexplained!' She glared at him.

'OK, OK, don't get sore. I kinda knew you'd take it like this, though there's no reason for you to get so uptight. If you must know, I specialised in geriatric medicine. It was pretty frustrating and I wanted to do more — to help make the back end of life as good as the rest.

'Then I suddenly got rich, was able to buy Eden Canyon, and put my theories into practice — provide a pleasant environment with lots of sunshine — and, hopefully, a longer, healthier life.'

He looked defensive. 'That's all there is. You've made it clear you don't approve of Eden Canyon, but that's your problem, not mine.' He added abruptly, 'I think it's time to go.'

As Josh drove her home, Juliette leaned back and, with half-closed eyes, watched his strong profile etched against the passing lights. Amazed by his revelation, she'd been stunned into silence as he'd paid the bill and collected the car from the valet parking.

Dr Svensen didn't fit her notion of Josh, the rich playboy and con-man. She had a lot of rethinking to do — about herself as well.

'Do I get invited in for coffee?' Lost in her thoughts, she hadn't noticed the car draw up outside the house.

'Could I keep you out? You do have keys, remember?'

'I'd rather you asked me in — but not to quarrel again.'

'All right. Maybe you deserve a cup of coffee.'

He hesitated. 'The truce is still on?'

'For the moment.' She made no move. 'Josh, how did you suddenly get so rich? The land and buildings must have cost a fortune.' She felt it was an important key to his actions.

He stiffened and, in the lamplight from the road, she saw him frown. 'Just lucky, I guess.' He got out quickly and came round to open the car door for her. Juliette knew he wasn't going to tell her.

In the house, he made himself at

home, taking over the coffee-making, moving around with easy familiarity, putting soft background music on the CD player. Juliette watched him carry the coffee tray into the living-room. It was nice to be waited upon.

'Thanks for this evening, Josh,' she told him. 'I've really enjoyed it. And thanks for telling me about yourself. You a doctor — that's a lot to take in.'

He shrugged. 'That's no big deal — but it's great to see you loosening up.' He came to sit by her. 'There's so much we could do together, if you'll let yourself go and learn to enjoy life.'

'I'm happy. I enjoy my work.' Juliette was defensive. 'I'm not the hedonist you seem to be.'

'I work hard, too — but there's still room for playing hard. There's so much more to life — so many exciting interesting things to do.'

'I've got to earn a living.'

'There are ways. Incidentally, you look five years younger tonight than when you first arrived.'

'Thanks a lot!'

Josh laughed at her and put down his cup. 'I've told you, you're beautiful — but now there's something else — a vitality — an awareness — a spark that wasn't there before. It suits you.' He pulled her to her feet, took her in his arms, and kissed her.

It was the perfect end to an enchanted evening. After a few moments, Josh raised his head and stepped back. His voice was husky. 'I'd better go. That extra spark — it's pretty exciting! You're hard to resist. I'll see you tomorrow.' He kissed her lightly on the forehead and left quickly.

Juliette couldn't decide whether she was sorry or glad.

5

Juliette slept late and dreamlessly, waking next morning to the ringing of the telephone. Sleepily, she tumbled out of bed, into the hallway, and picked up the receiver.

It was Josh's voice. Anger crackled down the line. The smile that had begun on her face froze there as her brain registered the tone. It was hideously reminiscent of the times in England when he, an aggressive, strange American, had called to complain about her neglect of her parents.

'What on earth, Julie,' he was saying now. 'I thought we'd got past feuding at the point. Why have I been sent this garbage from your solicitor? I had a message on the fax, from a firm of lawyers in Bristol, England.'

Juliette mobilised her sense of grievance. 'That's Phil, my cousin. I told him about your claim that you own my parents' house.'

'You're crazy.' It sounded like an expletive, he spoke so explosively. Exasperation was in every syllable. 'I do own it, it's not just a claim. Is it so impossible for you to trust me? Why didn't you tell me what you were up to before?'

Last night's warmth had entirely disappeared. There were no remnants left of it in either of them. Juliette felt the loss, but she heard herself respond, recognising her voice as the same cold one of their first acquaintance.

'Why should I tell you?' she snapped. 'You'd have tried to bulldoze me out of it. I've got to do what I believe is right. I have to.'

There was a pause at the end of the line, and when Josh spoke again he sounded calmer.

'OK, I accept that. Maybe you do, but the sooner this is cleared up, the better we'll get along.'

What did it mean — 'get along',

Juliette wondered — and how far was he expecting a relationship to go, if, indeed, there was one at all? Defensively, she asked, 'What are you going to do?'

'Do?' He was almost restored to his usual, good humour. 'Nothing — but can you come with me to the airport in a few days?'

'The airport — why?' She was bewildered, and wondered if he was planning to get rid of her, perhaps put her on a plane to England.

Patiently, as if to a small child, Josh said, 'To meet your cousin, of course. I rang him and we had a long talk. He sounded a reasonable sort of guy, so I invited him over.'

Juliette gasped. 'And he accepted? Just like that?'

'Just like that.' There was a trace of smugness in the voice which annoyed her, and she was not mollified when he added complacently, 'We'll sort it out — man to man.'

'The inference being that I'm just a

fussy female?' She was cross, but Josh refused to rise to the bait.

Abruptly, he asked, 'Will you come to California with me — just for a long week-end?'

Juliette's heart skipped a beat — what was he offering her? She kept her voice steady. 'Why California?'

'I'm due to speak at a conference in San Francisco.'

'You'll be working there, then?'

'Only part of the time. It's a great place. You'd love it.'

He was persuasive, but Juliette had made up her mind that Josh, on his own, showing her the sights, was one thing — but several days of American razzmatazz was not her style. Or was it? She really didn't know. Her life had always been dominated by just one goal, and even that had been her father's goal for her.

Now, she wasn't sure of anything any more — except that she wasn't going to let Josh Svensen distract her from her primary purpose — to discover the reason for the mystery surrounding her parents' last days.

She said coolly, 'No, thanks, Josh. I'd rather stay here until Phil comes. I'm only just beginning to get used to Arizona, and Eden Canyon is starting to interest me.'

Josh said evenly, 'OK, if that's what you want to do. I'll take Gina. She deserves a break, and it'll be useful having my secretary along.'

Juliette was aware of a wild desire to say that she'd changed her mind, but he'd put the phone down, and she was left to contemplate an emotion quite new to her — jealousy!

She was honest enough to realise that the thought of the slinky, dark-haired Gina, spending time away with Josh — on planes — at dinners — even at parties — was distinctly unpleasant. It was only with difficulty that she wrenched her mind away from it.

★   ★   ★

During the next few days, with Josh in San Francisco, she felt free to make a thorough exploration of Eden Canyon, and talk to as many residents as possible. It was oddly relaxing to know that she wouldn't be meeting that tall figure who had so much power to disturb her. Yet, without him, there was an emptiness as well. What had Bob Searle said? 'It's always quiet when he goes.' She missed that vital spark. Somehow, the sun wasn't so bright, nor the sky such an azure blue.

Explore as she might, she found nothing to suggest that Josh was engaged in anything other than doing good. No matter to whom she spoke, everybody seemed entirely content with life in general, and Josh in particular. Perhaps it was just as he'd said. Her parents had made unwise investments, with Josh taking a business opportunity, and her mother and father slipping quite peacefully out of their lives.

Why hadn't they sent for her, though? Josh had told her on the phone that they'd both had mild strokes — yet her mother had protested that all was well, and she shouldn't come. Juliette shook her head, tired of the circular pattern of her thoughts.

On the second day of Josh's absence, she drove the buggy to the health club. She had ten minutes on the various machines, then joined in an aerobics class for half an hour. She was amused to find that she, the youngest in the class, was the only one breathing hard. All the regulars, most of them twice her age, were ready to go jogging, or play tennis or golf, but she collapsed into the outdoor pool to swim a few, easy lengths.

When she finished, she went into the steaming Jacuzzi, where Mae Searle joined her. They sat together, enjoying being pummelled by the strong jets. Juliette turned her face to the sun, eyes closed. She felt hedonistic, totally relaxed. How different it all was from her working life at the hospital! For the moment, her worries melted away. She even forgot about the imminent arrival of Phil from the UK. She'd phoned him at home, but his answerphone gave her the message that he was 'out of town', so that was that. She wondered what Josh hoped to gain by asking her lawyer to Arizona. Why Phil was willing to come was easier to understand. There she was, in the wintertime, soaking up the sun under a brilliant sky by a palm-fringed pool. No-one could blame him for wanting a little of that.

'Is it always like this?' she asked Mae.

'Do you mean the weather?'

'No. I know it gets too hot in the summer. I mean the lifestyle.'

Mae slid into the foam and arched her shoulders to the massaging water.

'Well, don't forget Bob and I are retired. Lots of people do still work, though — and Eden Canyon is a great place to come home to.'

Juliette still found it difficult to believe that the contentment around her was genuine. She probed a little more. 'But there must be problems. It doesn't seem natural that everyone is so happy. Don't you feel cut off from the world here?'

'We are, I suppose, but it's good to be free of hassle. We worked hard all our lives in Los Angeles.' She reached over to switch the jets on again. 'Another five minutes?' Juliette nodded. 'Of course, you can't leave the world entirely. Even the residents here have their problems, but we help each other out, and . . . ' She hesitated. 'Josh doesn't like us to talk about it — but he's always ready to lend a hand.'

Juliette thought grimly that Josh hadn't been much help to her parents. All he'd done was appropriate their assets — but she didn't say that to Mae.

'Take Len and Barb now,' Mae continued. 'Barb has a heart problem. She needs a pace-maker, but they simply can't afford it. They foolishly let their medical insurance lapse.'

Juliette felt she'd spotted a flaw at last, and pounced. 'Well, that couldn't happen in Britain — even though we don't have constant sunshine. Mind you, we might have to wait a while for a pace-maker.'

Mae said, 'I probably shouldn't spill the beans, but Barb's going to get hers right away. Josh is paying.'

'Josh?' Juliette couldn't have been more astonished if she'd heard that it was the President of the United States who was supplying the money.

'Yes. He always tries to help anyone in need. He has a very patriarchal attitude to his residents.' Mae looked guilty. 'But I shouldn't have told — he hates these things being made public.'

Suddenly, Juliette's pre-conceived ideas about Josh Svensen and Eden Canyon were turned on their head. She needed time to sort out the notion that Josh, instead of being an opportunist, was actually philanthropic. How could she have been so wrong?

Mae's voice cut across her thoughts. 'I'm turning into a prune here, let's get out. Will you come back to the house for lunch?'

'Mae.' Juliette climbed out after her. 'How does Josh — how do you — find out about people's problems?'

Mae was towelling herself in a huge, cosy, white, bath towel, and Juliette picked one up, too. Mae said comfortably, as she dressed herself, 'Oh, we just look out for each other. And Josh looks out for us as well.'

Juliette's head was whirling — was it all patronisingly feudal, or was it just one man's way of providing a better way of life for the elderly? She no longer felt able to judge — but she certainly had much food for thought.

*　*　*

That night, she went to bed early with some books from the well-stocked library, half-hoping that Josh would ring from California. But he didn't — and why should he, she thought to herself. Undoubtedly, he would be busy — and enjoying his leisure moments with the lovely Gina. The thought gave her no comfort.

There was one more day before their return — and Phil's arrival. Juliette spent it by the poolside and in the recreational area bars and restaurants.

People knew who she was by now, and approached her all the time, talking kindly about her late parents. They spoke of how sociable they'd been, how friendly, party givers and goers, relaxed and outgoing! It was a picture of two people whom she found difficulty in recognising as her reserved, fairly rigid mother and father. Was this what Arizona, and Eden Canyon, had done for them? Perhaps they'd been right to move to America and all her qualms about it were misplaced. It seemed that all her ideas about everything were being toppled one by one, forcing her to rethink everything — most of all, her opinion of Josh.

She began, almost without knowing she was doing it, to look forward to his return. Her view of him had come full circle. First of all, the astonishing revelation that he had been a doctor, then the discovery that he genuinely cared about the people in his community, and wanted them to be comfortable and happy. She still had some reservations but, try as she would, she could find no evidence to the contrary.

Josh was still an enigma to her, but she was certain he was not the handsome, aggressive, and unfeeling man she had first seen him as. On further acquaintance, she had decided he was a practised charmer. That, too, was misguided, and now she was forced to acknowledge that he was a man of some depth — a man who cared. The question came, unbidden, into her head — did he care for her at all?

The thought startled her. What did it matter whether he did or not? If she'd ever seen a footloose, confirmed bachelor — it was Josh Svensen.

Phil's plane was due in Sky Harbour airport in the evening. Josh had promised to pick him up, providing he himself had returned from San Francisco. If he was not back, Bob would call for Juliette and take her to Phoenix to meet the flight.

As the time drew near, Juliette felt nervously excited. She dressed carefully in a white dress she'd bought at the mall. It was the perfect complement to her peachy tan. She was anxious to look her best, to show Phil she'd taken his advice and had relaxed and enjoyed the sunshine.

When the bell rang, she caught her breath, wondering whether it would be Bob or Josh. She was delighted to find that it was Josh.

He stepped inside, gave her an appreciative whistle and, to her surprise, picked her up exuberantly. Her skirt flared about her and the curtain of her hair swung across her face. 'Hey,' he said, 'I've missed you!'

For a fleeting moment, Juliette's defences went up again. 'Don't!' It came out more sharply than she had intended and she quickly added, half-apologetically, 'You're making me dizzy. Did you have a good time?' she then added politely.

'Fabulous! You should have been there.' His mood, obviously, was a buoyant one. Almost clinically, one part of her brain noticed that her pulse was racing, and she was alarmed at the power he possessed to excite her — and depress her, too. He and Gina had obviously had a good time!

Josh set her down. 'We'd better go. Your cousin's plane is running on time. I've called the airport.'

Blast! Juliette thought to herself. Why didn't I check that!

They drove out of the complex in the station wagon. Now she was more used to the landscape, she could pick out South Mountain and identify landmarks. Josh watched the road and said laconically, 'I suppose you've got Eden Canyon well figured out by now. Still looking for the serpent? Have you got past the barbed wire and armed guards?'

'I'm afraid I was prejudiced when I first arrived,' she confessed. However, if she had expected that to appease him, she was wrong.

'Prejudiced! I'd call it bigoted.'

Juliette began to feel defensive. She said hotly, 'What did you expect — you were just as bigoted as me!'

He was silent, seemed about to say something, and, then, disarmingly, turned towards her and grinned. 'Truce?'

She knew that there was much they had to talk about, but it was impossible not to respond to his overtures. 'Truce,' she said with an answering smile.

As promised, Phil's flight arrived on time.

Phil, looking remarkably fresh, enveloped her in a tight hug before putting out his hand to Josh. The two men seemed to find an instant rapport. It made them into a brotherhood from which she felt excluded. But the first meeting was not an appropriate moment to remind her cousin that the purpose of his visit was not just to have a holiday, but to investigate how his new 'buddy' had become the owner of the house that should have been hers. It would have sounded mean-spirited indeed in the hearty atmosphere around her.

As they drove out of the airport, Josh suggested a meal in town before taking Phil back to the complex. 'It's my guess you'd appreciate a place called The Stockyard. It's a historic, converted, cattle market.'

'Great!' Phil was enthusiastic. Juliette said nothing. It was going to be one of those evenings. A man's night, with huge steaks to prove it!

Josh was setting out to show the Englishman a good time, and Phil was an all-too-willing collaborator. After the meal, on the drive back, Josh told them that Mae had fixed a two-day trip to the Grand Canyon for all of them, starting the following afternoon.

Juliette could hardly believe her ears, but when she protested, Josh overruled her objections. 'He's here for a whole week. We'll have plenty of time for business after the trip. Give the poor guy a chance to enjoy himself first, Julie. Anyway, I've been wanting to show you our Number One Wonder of the World, so it'll kill two birds with one stone.'

It was irritating. Instead of being an ally, Phil appeared to have fallen straight into the opposing camp.

★ ★ ★

Next morning, her cousin slept late, and when he and Juliette did meet up, all he could talk about was the beauty of his surroundings. In fact, he was lyrical about them. 'The facilities are amazing. It's high time we had places like this in England.'

Josh, who had joined them for lunch, warned, 'You won't find hot sunshine at the Grand Canyon. Mae's booked us into a lodge in the village there. It'll be cold and you'll need jackets and sweaters.'

Together with the Searles, they left town on Interstate 17, heading north. As they travelled, Juliette thought that she understood at last what vastness meant. The immensity and timelessness of the desert panorama was awesome.

They stopped at Sedona. By then, she was growing used to the visual impact of deep-rose, monolithic out-crops. The scenery looked like a painted backcloth. Nonetheless, her first sight of the Canyon itself took her breath away. Josh had stopped the car at a viewing point. The air was bitterly cold as they trooped out to join a little bunch of tourists.

'Josh, it's incredible.' Involuntarily, she clutched him, wanting to feel something solid whilst looking at the enormous space at their feet and in front of them. He put his arm round her shoulders and seemed pleased at her reaction.

'Eighteen miles across and over a mile deep,' he said proudly. 'Look down.' Juliette watched the Colorado river wind its way along the deep, distant floor, but it was so far away it appeared a thin, jade ribbon. It was sunset, and deep, splashy colours were adding a compellingly-mysterious air to the scene. They watched in total silence.

It was beautiful and powerfully impressive, but as night fell, the high altitude and freezing air drove them back to the station wagon and on to the lodge where they were staying.

Mae was determined to keep a party atmosphere going and, after dinner, she and Bob described their white-river rafting trip through the Canyon, at the bottom of the deep gorge. 'That was in our young days. It can be tough going, but it was fun.'

The look she gave her husband, and his answering smile, brought a lump to Juliette's throat. There was a rapport between the Searles that was enviable, an understanding born of years of loving, devoted partnership. She couldn't remember her parents having such a deep relationship, though they'd seemed happy enough.

Josh looked across at her. 'Would you like to do that?'

'What?' Startled, Juliette's mind was still on the Searles.

'Come white-river rafting one day?'

I'd love to, her heart said, but there was still business to settle between them. 'I don't suppose I'll be passing this way again,' she said lightly, and Josh's mouth tightened.

The trip flashed by in a whirl of sightseeing. The next day they hiked some of the way down one of the Canyon trails, passing a mule train winding its way up, and in the afternoon flew over the Canyon to get an awe-inspiring, bird's-eye view. In the evening, they met up with a quartet of sun-tanned Californians, and Mae again made a party of it. Juliette had no chance of talking to Phil, who now appeared to be regarding the trip as an out-and-out holiday, with no business to be taken care of whatsoever.

'Come on, Juliette, this is the chance of a lifetime. I spend all my time dealing with the law. We'll get round to it. Promise!'

On the way back, they visited the Navajo Reservation, where she bought turquoise and silver jewellery from a wayside stall. It seemed odd to be buying Indian artefacts from 'Chief Yellow Horse' in the desert — and paying with a credit card!

After admiring the glorious colour of the Painted Desert, and the strange beauty of the Petrified Forest, Juliette was happy to call a halt and head back for Eden Canyon. She knew that when she returned to London, Arizona would seem like a dream — apart from all the photographs she'd taken.

Home in Eden Canyon, Phil and Josh now appeared to be lifelong friends, and it was with some misgivings that she overheard them fixing a 'business meeting.'

'Just Josh and me,' Phil said firmly when he saw her.

'Why am I excluded? It's my property you're talking about.'

'That's just it.' Phil looked at her sceptically. 'You're too involved. You wouldn't be objective enough. You've got yourself a lawyer — just let him do the work.'

For the moment, Juliette let the matter drop, but was eager to meet Phil afterwards to find out what had happened. As it turned out, she couldn't get him to herself until the night before he flew back to London — he and Josh seemed to have arranged to play squash or golf nearly every day.

In the evenings, they all went out to dinner together, either to a restaurant or to visit some of Josh's seemingly endless circle of friends, all eager to lavish hospitality on the young 'English pair.' When they got back to the house, Phil would protest he was too tired to talk, and he always slept late in the morning.

In desperation, Juliette pinned him down by insisting on cooking a special meal on his last night. 'Just the two of us,' she warned sternly, when he suggested inviting half of Eden Canyon — and Josh, of course.

'Well?' she asked eagerly. 'What did you find out? How did he get hold of the house?'

Phil, who must have foreseen that she would want to know, ate his meal in a leisurely fashion and seemed to be playing for time. Eventually, he put his knife and fork down and looked directly at her. 'Frankly, Juliette, I've had it out with Josh and it's all above board. He owns the house fair and square — in fact, he's been exceedingly generous. He bought the house, let them live there rent free, and gave them an annuity.'

'But my parents weren't paupers — you know they weren't. There's no way they could have got into debt sufficiently to hand over the deeds of their house. It's just not possible.'

Phil took his gaze from hers and seemed to be busy with his next course.

He said evasively, 'There isn't any use trying to contest anything. You'll just have to believe me. Josh told me everything and showed me all the papers I needed to see. You'll just have to drop it.'

'Drop it!' Juliette stood up, forcing Phil to look up at her. 'I don't understand. Ever since you came here, you've been in Josh Svensen's pocket. Well, he may have got round you, but he won't find me so easy to deal with. How could you, Phil? There's something fishy. It doesn't sound right. He's keeping something from me, and you know what it is!'

Phil sighed. 'I'm sorry. The question of the house is settled. It's his — fair and legally square. There's nothing more to do. About Uncle Joseph and Aunt Marjorie, that's his affair. He ought to tell you. It would certainly be better than — '

'Tell me what?' Juliette said eagerly, but Phil looked as though he regretted saying so much.

'Sit down.' When she reluctantly did so, he reached across and took her hand. 'I know it's hard,' he said sympathetically, 'but the only one who can explain is Josh himself. It's not my secret and I promised him . . . Anyway, my advice is to make him tell you. He'll do it — I know he thinks a lot of you.'

Her heart registered Phil's last remark, but, try as she would, she could get no more out of him except, 'Josh will tell you.'

6

After Phil had gone, Juliette felt lonely. It had been fun having him to stay, and the house seemed empty without his bubbling enthusiasm over anything and everything in Arizona. Whenever she was with him, she always felt the comfortable security of long familiarity. He was her family — all she had now. He'd also reminded her that she was due back in London in a week.

That thought, too, gave her a pang, making her realise the ease with which she'd slipped into the luxury, sunshine living of Eden Canyon. How resentful and bitter she'd been when she first arrived! All that had eased away — and yet there was still a question-mark hanging over the whole affair. 'Ask Josh, he'll tell you,' Phil had said. How many times had she done just that?

Since they'd returned from the

Grand Canyon trip she hadn't seen him, except for occasional glimpses at the health club, and then, or so it seemed to Juliette, he'd seen her, taken fright and vanished. She was honest enough to admit she missed him, and she was hurt to realise that he was deliberately avoiding her.

The question of her parents' personal effects was still to be resolved, and she'd have to decide what to do with them — a task she'd been putting off as long as possible. Time was running out, though. Josh couldn't avoid her for the rest of her stay, surely?

She phoned the office and Gina informed her, with a gleeful ring in her voice, that, 'Mr Svensen is unavailable at this time.'

'When will he be available?'

'He didn't say. Will you leave a message, Miss Jordan?' Gina was the only person on the whole complex to call her 'Miss Jordan'! Juliette was now so used to being called 'Julie' that even her own surname sounded strange. As for Juliette — that was a name from a different planet!

'No — yes — tell him' — she hesitated before making the final break — 'tell him Julie called. Ask him to ring back as soon as possible, please.'

The rest of the day she spent with Mae, who took her shopping to one of the more up-market malls. Juliette bought a few gifts for friends in England, and helped Mae choose some new leisure clothes. They'd practically decided to call it a day when Mae saw a stunningly-simple, blue silk dress. It figure-hugged the display model, was barely knee-length, and also had a plunging neckline.

'Now, isn't that just something?' Mae sighed.

Juliette looked doubtful, not liking to say the dress was a touch youthful for her friend.

'Goodness!' Mae read her expression. 'Not for me, obviously — for you. It's exactly the same colour as your eyes.'

'Mae, it's not me. Far too outrageous!'

'Try it on. Go on, just for fun.'

'I'd never wear it.' Juliette thought of her life back in London and couldn't think of any occasion where she'd wear such a sexily-sophisticated dress. Her own wardrobe was eminently sensible. She realised just how little time she'd had in the past for the luxury of a leisurely shopping trip such as this one she was enjoying with Mae.

''Course you will. Look, it's your size, too.'

'The price . . . ' Juliette was still reluctant.

'Oh, go on, spoil yourself for once. Bob and I are going to give you a farewell party, and you can wear it then. We'll all dress up for a change. It'll be fun.'

Juliette looked at Mae with affection. She'd grown very fond of the Searles since she'd been in Eden Canyon. Everything Mae did turned out to be fun — she had a zest for living which was contagious. More to please her than anything, she tried on the dress,

and couldn't believe that the sophisti-
cated woman she saw in the changing
cubicle was herself. Mae was right. The
colour matched her eyes perfectly, and
the soft silk folded round her body
voluptuously. To Mae's delighted satisfaction, she bought it.

She had supper with Bob and Mae,
and then went back to what she now
had to accept was Josh's house. As she
let herself in, the phone was ringing.
Her heart leaped. Surely, it could only
be Josh?

'Hi, Julie — Phil. Just to let you
know, I'm back home, and thanks for a
wonderful time.'

'Phil.' She tried to keep the disappointment out of her voice. 'Glad
you're safely back. It's lonely without
you.'

'Isn't Josh around?' Phil was surprised.

'No — should he be? I haven't seen
him at all since we got back from the
Canyon trip.'

'He hasn't spoken to you, then?'

'No. I just told you, Phil, I haven't seen him — so how could he have spoken to me? I think he's deliberately avoiding me. So your 'ask Josh' was a bit non-productive.'

'Blast!' Phil's exasperation was explosive. 'OK, Julie. I'll be in touch with you before you leave. Tell you what, I've got to be in London next week. You tell me your flight number and I'll meet you.'

'Would you? That'd be great. See you soon, then — and Phil . . . '

'Julie?'

'Thanks for coming over.'

'That was definitely my pleasure.'

Juliette barely had time to make a cup of coffee before the phone rang again. This time it was Josh.

'Julie — can I come over?'

'It's rather late. I was planning an early night.' She wanted to see him but, perversely, was annoyed he'd been so long in calling her.

'Come on, Julie, it's not that late. Look, I'm sorry I haven't called before.'

'You've been avoiding me, haven't you?'

There was a fractional pause. 'OK, I'll be honest. Yes, I have. I've got to talk to you. I've been trying to put it off, but — well — Phil's just called. He bawled me out — says I've got to do it.'

'Phil made you ring me?' she said in amazement. 'Well, you needn't have bothered. I'm not — '

'Hold on, hold on. Don't get back on that high horse of yours again. I wanted to call you, but what I have to tell you is pretty hard. I don't know how to do it.'

'What! Josh Svensen — the man who insisted I come to Arizona. The boss man himself — I don't believe it!'

It was true. She'd never seen Josh anything but fully, confidently, in command of any situation. His tentative hesitancy was quite new to her — and short-lived.

Almost before she'd finished speaking, Josh said, 'I've just had an idea.'

'What?'

'Julie — I'm asking you to trust me

again. I'd planned to make your last few days here pretty special — a night ride in the mountains, maybe some white-river rafting — that kind of thing. So you'd remember Arizona — and me — for a long time.'

Juliette's heart sank. It sounded like a very final farewell, and she didn't know if that was how she wanted it.

'Instead, I'm asking you to come on one more trip with me. It'd be great to see you tonight — right now — but I've a plan, and you'll need an early night. Go to bed now — and up at dawn. I'll pick you up at seven o'clock. Pack an overnight bag.'

'Where are we going?'

'Trust me — until tomorrow.'

'Josh, I've got to know where we're going. What'll I pack?'

He gave a splutter of laughter. 'You should know by now, anything goes around here. We're just hopping into the next state — Nevada. Pack your bag for Las Vegas. See you in the morning. Get some sleep now.'

He put the phone down before he heard Juliette's startled gasp. 'Las Vegas!'

Why on earth were they going to Las Vegas? Juliette rather mutinously threw some clothes into an overnight bag, half-inclined to ring Josh and tell him that she had no intention of going there. Las Vegas wasn't a top sightseeing priority for her, although its very name had a disreputably-glamorous ring.

Her image of the place was based on lots of old movies. Arizona, too, what she'd seen of it, sometimes seemed like one huge, Hollywood film set, with Eden Canyon the location of her particular film drama. Josh was an attractive-enough hero, that was obvious enough, though she doubted whether she measured up as a heroine! What she couldn't deny was that the prospect of spending time with Josh, annoyingly bossy though he could be, gave her a deliciously-warm sensation. She closed her bag then, as an afterthought, threw in the blue silk dress.

Josh was disgustingly cheerful at seven o'clock the next morning. 'Hi — you look wonderful. The sunshine has made a difference to you. I knew it would.' He had the smug air of someone who's been proved right. 'Sunshine and Arizona living. Great things! I knew you wouldn't regret your trip out here. We'll start straight away — have breakfast at Wickenburg — maybe take in the Hoover Dam . . .'

Juliette looked at him suspiciously. If she hadn't known him better, she'd swear he was nervous. He kept up a bright stream of travelogue-style information as they drove away in the ever-brightening sunshine. Once or twice, she quietly interrupted his increasingly-frenetic chatter with the reiterated question, 'Josh, why are we going to Las Vegas?'

His only answer was, 'Everyone has to go to Las Vegas once in a lifetime.'

In the end, she gave up, and enjoyed

the ever-changing scenery of rocks, desert and cacti, in the soft pinks, browns and olive-green colours she would always associate with Arizona — and with Josh. He pointed out the spiky Joshua trees — unique to the area, and she thought, yes, and I know another Joshua who's pretty unique, too.

In the early afternoon they drew near their destination, and Josh fell silent, a silence that became more intensely-brooding as the miles dropped behind them. The car crested a hill and Juliette gasped. The road stretched away before them, leading down to a vast plain — a plain that must have stood empty apart from the Indians for countless centuries.

In the last century, white men had constructed a city on that plain — an isolated, purpose-built city. It shimmered in the heat, its high-towered buildings stretching upwards.

Josh drew into the side of the road and stopped the car. 'There you are

— Las Vegas. That's where you'll find the answers to your questions.'

★   ★   ★

'It looks very interesting, but you'd no need to make a great mystery of it. Las Vegas is another 'wonder'. I'm looking forward to seeing it.' She knew that the unspoken words came from her heart were, that she'd go anywhere with Josh — if he asked her.

Juliette pushed the thoughts away. London was only a few days away — she had a career to follow, a life to live — and Josh Svensen clearly wasn't interested in her.

They drove down the hill towards the plain and, gradually, the grid system of Las Vegas streets drew them towards its glittering centre, and the main strip. Juliette looked around eagerly. There was atmosphere and frenetic bustle about the place which she found exhilarating, as the neon-flashing hotel signs followed one after another.

'We're staying in one of the hotels in the newer part — at Caesar's Palace.' Josh drove nonchalantly through the crowded streets and pointed out an ornate, white building, which reminded Juliette of a wedding cake with walkways. There was so much to see and absorb that she forgot Josh's enigmatic comment that here lay the answer to her questions.

No doubt he had his reasons for bringing her and he would tell her in his own time. More and more, it was enough just to be with him.

At the hotel, he handed over his keys and car to the valet parking service, took her elbow, and guided her towards the main foyer. The imposing marble entrance, with its statues and caged white tigers, made her draw her breath in sharply. It was completely over the top, yet another film set from another world. The elegantly-dressed mingled with tourists, wearing casual track-suits or shorts. She glimpsed discreet bars and lavish restaurants.

She drew in a breath. 'It's — just amazing. I've never seen anything like it.'

'You haven't seen anything yet.' His voice was grim, his brows knitted in a frown. 'Let's check in, and I'll show you what we've come to see.'

'This,' she indicated the busy glamour all around. 'Isn't this what we've come to see?'

'Oh, no. This is just the window dressing.'

He went up to the reception desk and spoke to the immaculately-turned-out young girl and, for a second, Juliette felt a twinge of doubt. He couldn't have booked a double room? Could he? Her heart plummeted at the thought that he'd brought her to Las Vegas simply to try to seduce her.

Then she was instantly ashamed of herself as his broad-shouldered figure turned away from the desk and held out a room key to her. 'We're on the sixth floor. We have adjoining rooms — but I doubt you'll sleep tonight. Las Vegas is open twenty-four hours a day. We'll freshen up, and I'll see you down here in the bar.'

Why did he continue to look so grim? Juliette felt the thrill and excitement of the place take her over. She was eager to see it all, to go to the famous casinos, to see fortunes lost and won.

Josh's strangely distant mood didn't dampen her excitement as she showered and changed. There was something electrifying about the atmosphere of the place which she sensed as soon as she'd seen it — a sort of feverish glitter which was new to her.

It was unnatural, and Juliette wasn't at all sure she approved, but there was no doubt she was affected by it. Without hesitation, she put on her new silk, blue dress.

Josh's own eyes widened as she came into the bar where he was waiting for her. 'I don't believe it.' His voice was awed. 'You look lovelier every time I see you. That dress — is — well!'

Juliette hoisted herself onto a bar

stool next to him and smiled. 'Glad you like it. Mae picked it for me.'

'A woman of impeccable taste.' He picked up her hand and held it to his lips. But still the frown persisted. It seemed that, whilst the holiday, party atmosphere of Vegas heightened Juliette's mood, it depressed Josh's. She'd never seen him look so serious. Angry, yes, but not like this — as if he had a huge weight pressing down on his powerful frame.

'What's the matter, Josh? Don't you find all this exciting? I'd like to take a look in the main casino.'

He groaned and put his head in his hands. 'I've seen it before — a bourbon on the rocks,' he muttered to the barman. To Juliette he said, 'What would you like to drink? They practically give it away here.'

'No, not now.' She was startled to see Josh gulp down the rough spirit in two swallows. He seemed to be falling apart before her. 'Josh?' she queried tentatively.

He slid off the bar stool and held out his hand. 'Right — I can't put it off any longer. Let's get it over with. Let me start by just clearing up one misconception. There's no main casino — every hotel has a casino. This whole town is devoted to gambling — twenty-four hours every day.'

'That's what it was built for, surely? If you disapprove so strongly, why have you brought me here? Isn't it part of the American scene?'

'Oh, sure.' Josh's voice was bitter.

'It's a pretty crafty money-spinner. State laws are different. You won't see any gambling in Arizona. Here in Nevada, it's legal. That's why thousands flock here every day — year in, year out.'

They came to the rooms where roulette, craps and black jack were being played. 'It looks quite civilised to me.' Juliette edged towards the green, baize-covered tables. 'We used to play roulette at home — at Christmas, years and years ago. It was fun.'

Josh threw her an agonised look as he took her arm and steered her towards the next room. Flashing lights, the rattle of coins from the fruit machines — the noise and lights made Juliette blink. He had to bend down so she could hear him. 'It's an addiction, Julie — can't you see?'

'It needn't be.' She looked up at him. 'It's like everything else — drinking, smoking, fast cars — you keep it under control.'

'How can you say that? You're a doctor, and you should know how easily anyone can be hooked — on anything. Once you start here, playing the machines or roulette, it's fatal. You can't stop gambling and you can end up losing everything.'

Juliette had only been half-listening, concentrating on watching the players at the tables. 'It doesn't have to be like that. I think I'll try the roulette.' Josh grabbed her arm sharply, his strong fingers digging deeply into her flesh. 'Ouch,' she gasped, 'you're hurting me.'

'Don't, Juliette, please. Don't! It's stupid. It's pure chance. There's no skill.'

She was surprised by his vehemence, and tried to break free from his restraining grip. 'Stop it, Josh. You're not my keeper. I'm going to try the roulette.

'You're always telling me to let my hair down. Have fun, you tell me. Well, now I'm going to. What's your problem?'

'Not like this — it's not for you.'

'How do you know what's for me? What's the point in coming to Las Vegas if I can't play the tables? I don't have a fortune to lose.' She shook free of Josh, and slipped into an empty chair at one of the tables.

A pretty waitress in a very short, fur-trimmed skirt asked her if she wanted a drink. Juliette shook her head, and the girl walked away, shooting an electronic, flashing yo-yo from her wrist with a practised flick.

'Have yourself a drink — it's all free

when you play at the tables.' A mournful-looking man, with a large stetson on the back of his head, spoke out of the corner of his mouth, his eyes fixed on the spinning wheel at the centre of the table.

Juliette had exchanged some money for round tokens on her way to meet Josh, and now placed some of them on numbers on the board. It was, as Josh had said, a game of pure chance, though she suddenly had a recollection of her father, over their family Christmas game, giving them all a lecture on working out odds, and mathematical probabilities. The memory made her smile as she placed her modest bets.

The croupier slid a glance round the table before making his final call. 'No more bets.' The wheel spun, and the steel ball bounced and ran in the counter direction before stopping in a numbered slot. 'Number 24.' He raked in chips and paid out winnings.

Juliette broke even on the first run of the wheel, then slowly began to win a little. Josh had followed her, and stood behind her chair. She could feel his tension. 'See, it's fun.' She laughed at him.

'That's enough. Let's have dinner now.' His face was stern, and yet he looked strangely apprehensive.

'Why don't you have a bet?'

'No.' His refusal was curt and emphatic. Juliette shrugged. 'Come on,' he insisted.

She sighed. It wasn't worth an argument. She was enjoying herself, but dinner with him would be more fun. 'One last spin.' She put all her winnings on zero.

'That's what they all say,' he snapped. 'Leave it, please.'

The ball stopped — at zero. Juliette gave a squeal of delight. 'Josh — I've won.' She remembered, from her childhood, that on the zero bet the bank paid 35-1. She gathered up her winnings and stood up. 'That's that, Josh. When you're ahead — that's the time to stop. Let's eat.'

Relief relaxed the tension lines of his face and, as they moved away from the table, he put his arms around her. 'You don't want to play some more?'

'Heavens, no. I just wanted to try it — see what happens. Watch the people.'

'And what do you see?'

'A lot of people having fun and new experiences. Just because I think it's a crazy way of having fun doesn't mean others shouldn't enjoy it. Most people have a blind spot — a weakness — maybe an addiction.' She looked up at him curiously. 'You're supposed to be the hedonist. I'm surprised you don't want to play.'

'I think I've learned my lesson with that.' Josh's blue eyes were serious and the tension had returned to his face. 'Come on. We'll have dinner, and I'll tell you about it.'

He took her hand and they left the casino. Outside, it should have been dark, but the blazing neon of thousands of flashing signs made short work of the night sky. In whichever direction

Juliette looked left, right, or upwards, bright colours winked crazily on and off. It was garish, glitzy, dreadful — and fascinating. 'Wowee!' Juliette couldn't help it.

Josh smiled. 'Well, well. Something's made an impression at last.'

7

Josh had found a comparatively-quiet restaurant off the main strip, where they could forget the feverish world outside.

Juliette knew he was going to tell her something important, and a knot of apprehension in her stomach banished hunger. She ordered a salad.

Josh appeared to have lost his appetite, too. After a cursory glance at the menu, he chose a small steak and baked potato. He waved away the wine list. 'Mineral water, please. What I'm going to say doesn't give me any cause for celebration. Maybe later.'

There was a basket of bread rolls on the table, and Juliette picked one up, beginning to shred it nervously.

Josh cleared his throat. 'I brought you here on impulse, after Phil phoned. He insisted I tell you the whole story about your father. I never wanted to, but he said it's not fair to keep you in the dark any longer.'

'Phil! What is it to do with him? What is it, for goodness' sake?' Her blue eyes pleaded, and she put out a hand to touch his wrist. 'Please.'

'Phil's your family — he's concerned, too.' He caught her hand and held it before he spoke again. 'You once asked me where I got the money for Eden Canyon. Why I gave up medicine.'

'That's your business. I don't care.' She shook her head impatiently.

'It's kinda related. It'll help, maybe, to hear the full story.'

'Go on, then.' Juliette was terse.

'I had a friend at Medical School — Ed Halpern. He was a mathematical genius — a walking computer. A good poker player who always won by working out the odds. A phenomenal memory and grasp of figures.'

Juliette took her hand away and moved restlessly.

'There's a reason for telling you

about Ed,' Josh anticipated her inter-ruption. 'Be patient.' The waitress arrived with their food, but he made no attempt to eat. 'Ed and I both qualified. He specialised in obstetrics and gynae-cology — his dream was to set up his own maternity unit — mine to build a place like Eden Canyon. All fantasy. Our folks were well off, but not millionaires!

'We talked a lot about it and, one day, Ed told me his crazy scheme. He'd been thinking about it for years. We'd play the tables at Vegas, using Ed's foolproof system — we'd make a fortune! I thought he was mad, but he was a pretty charismatic character, and I went along with it.' He paused, cut a small piece of meat, and put it in his mouth. 'Eat your salad.' He nodded towards her plate.

She shook her head and pushed it away. 'And did you? Make a fortune, I mean. You said it was all a matter of chance.'

'It is — to the amateur. Thousands

have tried it — few do it. We did.' He smiled reminiscently. 'I'll never forget that night. Ed played until dawn. We'd raised as much cash as we could beforehand. Ed was determined to break the bank or lose it all.'

'And you won?'

'We won,' he agreed sombrely, 'but I guess I lost a stone in weight and aged ten years in that one night. Around dawn, we walked away with a pretty sizeable sum.'

'Surely not enough for Eden Canyon and a maternity unit?'

'Not at first. We needed more collateral to borrow from the bank, but phase two of Ed's scheme was the winner. He took all the money we won and played the stock markets. Believe me, if you know what you're doing there — and Ed did — you can really make a killing. It was a pretty tense time, but in two years we built up a small fortune.

'Sometimes we shifted millions of dollars in one day — I still get nightmares about that. But we finally made it. Ed has his unit in California, and I have Eden Canyon. I was lucky. Land was cheap in the desert, and I gradually bought more and more, until it's as you see it today.' He ended defensively, 'You may not approve of the means, but I'm convinced the end is justified.'

'I neither approve nor disapprove. I just can't see what it's got to do with my parents.' She was puzzled.

Josh fixed his eyes on her face, speaking more slowly. 'When your parents came out from England, we hit it off straight away. I just loved them. So English, polite, reserved and cautious. After a month at Eden Canyon, they were different people. Mr and Mrs Jordan became Joe and Margie — to everyone.' Juliette shook her head in disbelief. 'It's true — you've been asking around, so you know it is.

'Maybe it was the sunshine, the relaxed lifestyle, but they blossomed, Julie, exactly as you've done. You've changed, too — and I don't want to hurt you.' He took her hand again. 'I got to know them well — and I also got to know their daughter. They were so proud of you — I was fascinated. I knew just about everything there was to know about you — even when you cut your first teeth, took your first steps . . . '

'Oh, no!' Juliette's cry of embarrassment was loud enough to startle nearby diners. 'Why did you encourage them?' she snapped. 'That's awful!'

'No, it's not. They had photographs to mark every stage of your life. I loved you as a pony-tailed youngster on a horse! Graduation day! A very serious young doctor in a white coat, and I really fell for that stunning Julie in a bikini . . . '

'That was the last holiday I had with them — in Spain. They shouldn't . . . you shouldn't — '

He touched her hand gently. 'The trouble was, I began to fall in love with that girl Margie and Joe brought to life for me. I couldn't get you out of my head. I'd plague your mother to tell me more about you. She so loved to talk about her beautiful daughter, it was easy. The thing I couldn't figure out was why you never visited them at Eden Canyon. I asked them when you were coming, and they always put me off. 'When she's established a career', or, 'She's so busy right now, she'll be over some day'.'

Juliette hung her head. 'I should have come, I know it now, but so many times they put me off in the same way. I see the tragedy, now it's too late.'

'So,' Josh continued, 'I built up this fantasy picture of a lovely, caring daughter who, for whatever reason, couldn't make it out to see her folks — and Margie and Joe seemed happy — '

'But . . . ' Juliette interrupted.

'This is the hardest bit,' Josh cut in quickly. He picked up his glass and drained it, put it down, and held both her hands across the table. 'I made the mistake of telling Joe all about Ed.'

'I don't see — '

'Julie — your father was a compulsive gambler. It ruined his life in England and, I'm afraid, that's why he lost his money here in the States.'

Juliette snatched her hands away. 'Don't be ridiculous, you're making it up. How dare you say that! It was you. I was right — you conned my father into giving you his house and money. Then, when I arrive to find out what went on, you make up this stupid story . . . ' Her voice rose, and she made to get up from her chair.

'Sit down,' Josh said sharply, his eyes stern and commanding. 'I never wanted you to hear this, but you'll hear it now. You're not thinking straight. Get your facts right. You forget the most important one — I begged you to come over here. Why would I do that if I had deceived your parents?'

'But — it can't be true. Dad never gambled in his life. We always had plenty of money.'

'Why did they leave England?' Josh's voice was gentler now.

'I don't know. It was a sudden decision. I never understood.'

'Because Joe was heavily in debt. He'd gambled on the stock exchange — and lost. But that's why he was so interested in Ed's story. I'll never forgive myself for telling him. It all started again. I had no idea — until it was too late. Then, when Phil told me about the past — '

'Phil! He knew — all those years?'

'I'm afraid so. There's been a family conspiracy of silence. You were such a precious gift in your parents' late years, they couldn't bear the thought that you'd be hurt or disillusioned.'

The waitress came to clear their plates. 'Wasn't it good?' She looked worriedly at the food — barely touched.

'Fine. We're just not very hungry. I'm sorry,' Josh apologised. 'Just coffee, please.'

'Sure thing.' She was reassured by his smile.

Juliette was silent, trying to absorb

what Josh had said, trying to remember the past, pick up clues . . .

He went on, 'Just before she died, Margie told me the whole story. Joe fought all his life to conquer his addiction and, for a time, after you were born, he kept it more or less under control. He built up a business — lived for you — maybe through you.'

Juliette admitted, 'That's true — he did.'

'Then, when you left home for college, he started gambling again — and couldn't stop. He lost a lot of money, faced bankruptcy. Your uncle, Phil's father, bailed him out. Your mother had some money of her own, and they decided a completely fresh start would be the best thing in as different an environment as they could get. And for a while it worked.'

'Why didn't they ask me to help?' Juliette's cry was anguished.

Josh's own face mirrored her distress. 'You know that,' he answered quietly. 'You were their pride and joy, and they decided nothing should get in the way of your career. Their problems were secondary — you mustn't be worried. Maybe they were wrong, but that's how they were. And, you must believe me, they had a truly wonderful time at Eden Canyon. It was only the last months which were sad.'

'Tell me.'

'Someone fixed up a trip to Las Vegas. It's pretty common — being one of the USA 'wonders.' Your father went. Three days later he came back. He'd lost everything — and, even worse, there was a big debt — he'd used the house to cover a promissory note. I know — ' He paused at her horror-struck expression.

'It's incredible, but that's what happened. Your mother was devastated. I wanted to get you over here, but she wouldn't hear of it. Even when they were ill they didn't know I'd sent for you. I couldn't believe you could be so callous as not to come. My image of you — my dream girl — collapsed in a heap. I was so glad when you showed me your mother's letters.'

He looked deep into her eyes before he went on. 'After the Vegas trip, your father got sick. I think he just lost heart. We tried everything.'

'And you bought the house?'

'I had to — to pay the debt.'

'Why? They were almost strangers. And you must have made them an allowance to live on.'

Josh looked uncomfortable. 'Where's that coffee?' he muttered.

'Don't hedge.' Juliette was sharp. 'Why did you do it?'

He made a great play of looking around for the waitress, who was already on her way with the coffee.

'It wasn't like that.' He slowly spooned in sugar and stirred. 'Joe and Margie were my friends — and I felt guilty about telling them Ed's tale. I'm sure that got your dad thinking. They weren't short of money, but Ralph, your uncle, kept them on a fairly tight rein financially.'

'But you can't take on all the financial problems of everyone who lives in Eden Canyon.

'I don't. I've told you, your parents were my friends — and they loved Eden Canyon so much. I wish you could have seen them here.'

'I've got a good picture. Everyone says the same thing.'

'They faded away peacefully and quietly, and they died willingly, Julie. I guess that must hurt you, but they were desperate that you shouldn't think badly of your father. They never lost that bright vision of you at the top of your profession — a brilliant professor of surgery!'

'I'm not sure I want that now.' Juliette sat back, all anger drained. It did make sense, but she'd been too single-minded to see it. Her mother's constant, worried frown, her father's frequent absences from home, always explained as business trips. Even the Christmas roulette games!

If only they could have talked to her,

but, as Josh said, that's how they were. She needed time to come to terms with it all. There was a long silence before she said simply, 'I think I'd like to go home now.'

'To London?' Josh's shoulders dropped.

'No — Eden Canyon.'

'It's too late tonight, but we'll leave early tomorrow. Maybe I shouldn't have brought you here, but I thought if you could see how it is — the addiction — it would be easier to understand your father.'

'I'm grateful — for lots of things, Josh. For what you did for my parents — for showing me Eden Canyon — Arizona.' Her dark eyes were eloquent as she looked at him. 'I'm getting a whole new perspective on things.'

'I'm glad.' Josh's voice was husky. 'Julie — don't go back to England. Stay here.'

She caught her breath. There was nothing she would love more than to stay with Josh, but, without him, there could be no future for her in Arizona. 'I have to work at something. I have a job at the hospital. I can't laze around lotus-eating for much longer.'

'There's plenty to do in Eden Canyon.'

'You're surely not offering me a job? What as — resident doctor?'

'Not a bad idea at all. Yes, I am offering you a job — but it's one for life. I want you to marry me.' He leaned forward, and their faces were almost touching.

'I love you, Julie. I've probably been in love with you ever since your mother showed me your graduation photograph. All the time I tried to get you over here — for your parents — I always knew it was for me. As soon as you came, even though I was hopping mad, I knew I was right. I was in love with you. And every day you've been here I've fallen more and more in love with you.

'That's why it's been so hard — to tell you about your folks. I just hated to hurt you.'

Juliette felt her eyes smart with tears. Josh loved her! Wanted to marry her! It was incredible — and she knew now that she could acknowledge what had been in her heart ever since she first set eyes on him. She knew she loved him!

His blue eyes were anxious. 'Julie? You will marry me, won't you?'

'Of course I will. I love you, too.'

He leaped up and swept her into his arms and kissed her — to the amused delight of other diners. 'Let's get out of here. I've had enough of Vegas. We will go back tonight. Drive through the desert. I can't kiss you properly here! And we'll go back to London together to give your notice in. I'm not letting you out of my sight until we're married.'

They checked out and drove across the desert, turning their backs on the day-bright city. When they were far enough away from the garish lights, with only starry night and silence around them, Josh stopped the sleek, silver car and held out his arms. Juliette

went into them with a sigh of joy and turned her face eagerly towards his. As she felt the warm pressure of his mouth, and his strong arms around her, she knew she had finally come to her own Eden in Paradise and would live there for ever, happily, with her true love.

THE END

We do hope that you have enjoyed reading this large print book.

Did you know that all of our titles are available for purchase?

We publish a wide range of high quality large print books including:
Romances, Mysteries, Classics
General Fiction
Non Fiction and Westerns

Special interest titles available in large print are:
The Little Oxford Dictionary
Music Book, Song Book
Hymn Book, Service Book

Also available from us courtesy of Oxford University Press:
Young Readers' Dictionary
(large print edition)
Young Readers' Thesaurus
(large print edition)

For further information or a free brochure, please contact us at:
Ulverscroft Large Print Books Ltd.,
The Green, Bradgate Road, Anstey,
Leicester, LE7 7FU, England.
Tel: (00 44) **0116 236 4325**
Fax: (00 44) **0116 234 0205**

THE THEATRE ON THE PIER

Heather Pardoe

Escaping a disastrous relationship, Llinos Elliot moves to North Wales. There she gets a job as administrator with a children's community theatre, 'The Theatre on the Pier'. Llinos loves her job, and is drawn to Adam Griffiths, the artistic director. But she soon finds her past catching up with her, putting not only her and Adam, but the very existence of the theatre, in danger. Can Llinos overcome her past to find true happiness?